Granite Lake Wolves

Wolf Signs

Wolf Flight

Wolf Games

Wolf Tracks

Wolf Line

Wolf Nip

Takhini Wolves

Black Gold

Silver Mine

Diamond Dust

Moon Shine

Takhini Shifters

Copper King

Laird Wolf

A Lady's Heart

Wild Prince

A full list of Vivian's print titles is available on her website

www.vivianarend.com

PRAISE FOR VIVIAN AREND

"Vivian Arend does a wonderful job of building the atmosphere and the other characters in this story so that readers will be sucked into the world and looking forward to the rest of the books in the series."
~ *Library Journal*

"Steamy and sweet complete with a whole host of colourful side characters and enough sub-plots to get your teeth into. A fab read!"
~ *Scorching Book Reviews*

"There's a real chemistry between the characters, laced with humor and snappy dialogue and no shortage of steamy sex scenes to keep things lively. The result is an entertaining, spicy romance."
~ *Publishers Weekly*

Silver Mine is an outstanding story. The author creates a world that invites readers for the ride of their lives."
~ *Coffee Time Romance Reviews*

Arend offers constant action and thrills, and her characters are so captivating and nuanced that readers will have a hard time guessing who the villains really are.
~ *RT Book Reviews*

WOLF GAMES

NORTHERN LIGHTS EDITION

VIVIAN AREND

This is a work of fiction. Names, characters, places, and incidents either are the product of the author's imagination or are used fictitiously, and any resemblance to any persons, living or dead, business establishments, events, or locales is entirely coincidental.

1

———

June, Liard Hot Springs, Northern British Columbia

aggie hesitated as the boardwalk underfoot blurred.

"You okay?"

She nodded but grabbed another couple of pills from her backpack and chased them down with a few swallows of water. Her dizzy spells had grown more frequent. Was she really okay? Not yet, but the cure might be closer than before.

"You're seriously freaking me out. If I didn't know better I'd suspect you were popping something other than herbal remedies." Pam blocked her path and looked her over sternly. Finally satisfied, her friend grabbed Maggie's gym bag off her shoulder. "Since you insist you need to soak instead of just hitting the sleeping bags, I'm your Sherpa. You concentrate on walking. I don't want to have to figure out how to carry your sorry ass again."

Maggie laughed faintly. "Hey, it only happened one time."

"Yeah, once was enough. You may look like a twig, but you're damn heavy." Pam winked, then offered her elbow. "Do you need an extra hand? I'm here for you."

"I'm fine. Really. I just need a couple hours floating. Liard Hot Springs is a little bit of heaven on earth."

They walked in companionable silence down the worn boards of the four-foot-wide path leading into the bush of northern British Columbia, summertime heat rising around them. Beautiful weather had followed them the entire trip from Vancouver. The bright green colours of new growth in the marsh grasses on either side of the boardwalk made a soul-refreshing break from the concrete that had filled Maggie's world for far too long. Towering spruce trees, the brilliant blue of the June sky, crisp clean air—all of it slipped into her blood like a tonic. A tightly locked knot in her core loosened, and for the first time in almost a decade she didn't resist.

Her wolf stirred.

Oh God, that felt amazing. Maggie stopped in midstride and closed her eyes to let the sensation roll over her. Surround her. Like an icy cold barrier had broken open a crack, shivers trickled through her limbs. Electric. Delightful.

"Shit, are you having a seizure or something?" Pam clutched her arm and shook her gently. Maggie fought to keep from baring her teeth. Because wouldn't that just freak the human out to learn there were some secrets even best friends didn't share.

They were close to the changing shelters, rustic wooden squares built of upright rough-cut timber. Splashing noises trickled to Maggie's ears as she fought down the longing in her limbs she refused to answer. "I'm just tired. Let me get into the water."

"Fuck that. You have...drown. Just...careful...hell." Pam's voice faded in and out of Maggie's range of hearing. It was the most confusing thing. Her friend's lips continued to move, but the words disappeared. All that remained was this loud buzzing noise, like a swarm of horseflies. Maggie tried not to laugh at the funny expression on Pam's face as she waved her arms frantically and flapped her hands at someone racing around the corner of the decking surrounding the hot springs.

Someone? Maggie peered harder through the fog drifting in front of her eyes. That wasn't a person, it was a walking wall. Whoa, the man was huge. Dripping wet from head to toe, gorgeous tattoos seemed to writhe on his torso as he reached for her.

Hmm...he smelt delicious.

Strength.

Safety.

Sensations of happiness and contentment stole through her chaotic thoughts. Her feet didn't seem to be touching the ground anymore, and the world bounced gently. She cracked open one eye to gaze around. Above her, the trees rotated, and a small cloud chased across the sky in a blur. Warmth surrounded her up to her neck and she let out a contented sign. Her head rested on something firm yet soft, and she nuzzled against it tighter. A steady banging echoed in her ear, somehow reassuring.

And that scent? *Oh yeah.* She drew a deep breath, filling her nostrils and enjoying the way her mouth watered. It was like sitting down to a well-cooked rib-eye steak, with all her favorite side dishes. The sweetest dessert, followed by a dozen shooters. Maggie took another leisurely inhalation before snuggling closer to the thumping noise.

~

Erik caught sight of the women as they strolled down the boardwalk, one of them swaying from side to side.

He laughed quietly. He'd have a set of slightly tipsy females to keep an eye on while they soaked. The youth from his pack traveling with him played off to the left in the cold pool section of the natural hot springs. Splashing and hooting and the sounds of carrying-on filled the air.

Wolves—they were such children.

He waded through the water toward the deck. The woman on the right looked familiar. Petite, blonde, youthful features. If she'd been hugely pregnant he would have sworn it was Missy, the Omega for his pack, although she wasn't the kind to get falling-down drunk.

It appeared he was about to meet his reason for driving south sooner than expected. It had to be Maggie weaving toward him.

He watched with growing concern as the women's forward motion slowed. It wasn't just a tipsy ramble anymore—something seemed wrong. Erik grabbed the edge of the railing, wondering if he should offer assistance.

"Oh shit, help, someone. Damn it. Help." The brunette waved her arms, the frantic motions drawing his attention to the other woman as she wavered on unsteady limbs. He leapt out of the water, droplets spraying from his body to soak the worn boards underfoot. Long strides carried him down the boardwalk just in time to catch the blonde before she collapsed.

His world shifted out of line to the left.

Shocks—like small electrical connections—registered where their bodies touched. Trickles shot through his limbs and up his spine. Tingling. Snapping. *Oh hello*, it felt completely and wonderfully right.

"Thanks—she's been getting dizzy, and I didn't want her to collapse and hurt herself." The dark-haired woman kept rambling, but the entire focus of Erik's attention centered on the beautiful female he held in his arms. He turned and walked back to the water, taking the steps while still cradling her close.

"What the hell are you doing? She's passed out. She needs to recover and—" The friend followed him down into the pool, tugging at his elbow.

"—stay warm. Don't worry, I've got her."

Erik had no intention of letting her go. Ever. But that probably wasn't what this other woman wanted to hear. He settled on one of the submerged benches scattered through the natural pool and rearranged his mate in his arms, her head resting on his chest. The sensation of her cheek on his bare skin made his whole body react.

His mate.

Incredible. After all these years of waiting and longing, she'd dropped into his arms out of the blue. For now, knowing she actually existed was enough to make him want to shout in delight.

Except, he didn't do shouting.

A rather piercing voice broke through his intense concentration and he remembered the friend, now glaring at him with suspicion.

He held out his free hand. "Erik Costanov, from Alaska."

The brunette ignored his hand. "Pam. I think you should let me take care of my friend now."

"I've got her."

"I noticed. I'd prefer it if you weren't holding her. Just take her over to the stairs. I'll help—"

"Relax. I won't hurt her." *I'm going to care for her for the rest of my life.* The thought sent shots of pleasure through his system. Finally. His mate.

"Really, I'm not comfortable—"

"She's comfortable."

It was true. The small armful of blonde snuggled in tighter, and Erik's heart swelled. Hmm. This was going to be wonderful. Except for the fainting bit. They'd have to figure out what was causing it and—

A splash of water struck him in the face. "Hey, buddy. Thanks for stopping Maggie from hitting the deck, but I'll take over now. Got it?" Pam tugged on his arm, causing small waves to splash everywhere.

Erik took a deep breath. Maggie. He'd been right. He laughed at the irony. All this time waiting, and his mate was the sister of his Omega. Why hadn't he known?

"Look, mister, I don't know what the hell you think is so funny—"

A soft groan rose from Maggie. "Pam, can you stop the shouting for a sec? You're killing me here."

Oh hell, even her voice made his body sing. She squirmed and he carefully cradled her against him, keeping her head above water.

Pam leaned over and looked her in the eye. "Maggie? Can you hear me?"

"Are you kidding? They heard you in Vancouver. Stop screaming, my head hurts enough already. If you want to be helpful, I'm thirsty."

"There's a bottle of water in my backpack. Pass her to me and go get it," Pam demanded, giving him the evil eye.

Bossy chick. Erik smiled. It was good to know his mate

had a friend who wanted to protect her, although he would provide all the protection needed from here on out.

Conveniently, the teens traveling with him had gathered close, curious to see what was happening.

"Cody, grab some water for our friends," he ordered. The boy nodded and raced for their cooler on the deck.

Maggie wiggled again, and Erik savoured the weight of her on his lap. The brush of her skin increased his pleasure. The sweet smell of her natural perfume filled him with the dire need to taste her skin.

Cody handed over a bottle of water, and she guzzled most of it down.

Pam watched him like an overeager chaperone, her gaze dancing around the pool area. She seemed concerned there were now four strange males crowding her and Maggie, and Erik motioned for the boys to step away.

"Did I pass out?" Maggie spoke soft and slow, her words barely audible.

"You weren't out cold, but neither were you were coherent. Do you need your pills?" Pam asked.

Maggie leaned back on his chest, her head turned slightly so the warmth of her breath brushed him. "No pills. This is heavenly. I haven't been this relaxed for months."

Erik smiled. She knew him too. Her body already sensed they were meant to be together.

The friend glared harder, her eyes narrowing in suspicion as if Erik were somehow making Maggie respond like a puppet. "Umm, Mags? If you're feeling up to it, you want to come sit over here with me?"

"Nope. Comfy here." Her words slurred.

He peered over the top of her head to see her eyes were closed. Long dark lashes rested on milky white skin. He admired the contrast against his darker colouring where her arm rested on his biceps. She draped herself over him without shame, accidentally grinding her hips against his groin and his cock woke.

Oh yeah. Getting to the intimate part of their relationship would be fine as well.

She moved lazily, lifting her arms to stretch. Her fingers missed brushing his cheek by inches, and he refrained from leaning closer to let her stroke him. Her wonderful scent lingered in the air and he inhaled deeply in appreciation. *Hmm.* All those days of watching his Alpha pair care for each other brought his anticipation for this moment to a fine peak. So this is what it felt like to find the missing part of your soul.

Maggie smacked her lips. "Is there a snack bar here?"

"Are you hungry?" Pam hovered closer.

"No. Just trying to figure out what that fabulous smell is. Why were you shouting?"

Pam pointed over Maggie's shoulder and sniffed. "He's being stubborn, and I really wish you'd stop sitting on him."

The steady beat of his mate's heart sped up. She reached under the water and her fingers slipped over the bare skin of his thigh, sending another thrill along his nerves. Oh hell yeah, the connection rocked between them.

"Pam? Where am I?" Maggie twisted in slow motion to stare up at him, the deep blue of her eyes flashing with recognition for an instant before she opened her mouth.

And screamed.

2

Maggie scrambled off his lap so fast she slipped, her feet skidding on the soft rocks at the bottom of the outdoor pool. The towering mass of man in front of her caught her easily before her head went under.

"Take it easy, Maggie. You're safe." He settled her on her feet and stepped back. The bright smile in his eyes and on his face made something inside her twist and leap for joy at the same time. Her wolf fought to be free and her stomach clenched in reaction.

He was a werewolf. She recognized him from pictures Missy had sent online over the past couple of years. He was the damn Beta for her sister's pack and he was here in Liard Hot Springs pool and her wolf lusted for him. *Great. Let's just jump in with two feet, shall we?* After avoiding everything to do with wolves for years, the first one she met had to turn her crank. Movement to his side caught her attention as a group of young men approached.

"Erik? Is that Maggie?"

"Of course she is. She looks like her sister. Hi, Maggie, welcome to the North."

The three youths continued to advance, all talking at once. Maggie backed up rapidly, slamming into Pam's side. Oh God, there were four wolves in front of her. Panic rose and she pushed it down. She had to get over her fears.

"Do you know these people?" Pam wrapped a protective arm around her shoulders.

Erik nodded. "We're friends of her sister. We were supposed to meet you in Whitehorse."

Pam looked around pointedly.

One of the boys spoke up. "We begged Erik to bring us to the hot springs. It's been a while and with the Games starting soon and us not being able to participate yet he—"

"Games?"

Erik broke in, his gaze locked on Maggie. She kept eye contact only through sheer will power. "We were supposed to meet tomorrow. It's just a lucky break we're here at the same time. Are you okay now, Maggie? Do you need me for anything?" The heat in his eyes let her know his offer was wide open to interpretation.

Strip and let me ride you. Maggie felt her skin flush, and it wasn't from the heat of the water around them. Was this really happening to her? She shook her head and finally noticed she still wore her shorts and T-shirt over her swimsuit. "Let me get changed and then we can talk."

Pam held her elbow and together the two of them slogged their way out of the pool to the change house, a trail of water following them. Maggie snickered as she glanced at her friend.

"Sorry for making you take a swim with all your clothes on."

Pam waved a hand. "Forget it. You feeling better?"

"Yeah. I think I'll be okay now."

"Good." Pam pulled off her shirt and wrung it out. She peeked out the door of the change shelter and snuck back to whisper. "Are these guys safe? Do you really know them?"

Maggie sat on the bench to wrestle her wet runners off her feet. "I know *of* them. I've never met them but my sister did say someone would come escort me from Whitehorse to Haines. She didn't want me driving by myself after I drop you off at the airport."

"She couldn't come? At least so you'd know they were who they say they are?"

Maggie snorted. "From the sounds of it, Missy doesn't fit in a car very well right now. The soon-to-arrive twins are making her life difficult and I certainly don't expect a pregnant woman to sit for a four-hour trip just to make me feel better. Don't worry, I recognize Erik. He works with my brother-in-law's family. He's a wilderness guide."

"He's a tank."

A burst of laughter escaped her. "He is rather large, isn't he? Rather...yummy, too."

Pam raised her eyebrows. "Really? Crap, Mags, I haven't seen you express interest in anything male for..." She stopped and frowned. "Have I ever seen you express interest in a guy?"

Maggie hit her. "Stop it."

"If he's someone you trust, fine. I just think it's weird that of all places to meet, it's out here in the wilderness. I thought the North was this vast wild land, with wild creatures running free everywhere. Not a social club."

They stepped out of the change shelter and Maggie took a deep breath as the three young men did cannonballs into the lower pool, chasing each other like puppies. "Oh, I think there's plenty of wild animals around, if you know where to look."

ERIK WATCHED CONTENTLY as the youths finally lured Pam to another section of the pool to play a game, leaving him alone with Maggie for the first time. She sat on the narrow edge of grass at the side of the pool, dangling her feet in the water. The thick underbrush of the wilderness behind her framed her sweet body. She clutched the mossy surface with her fingers, head averted, but he knew she was looking him over.

He stood from where he'd sat, neck deep in the hottest part of the pool. Slow, even steps brought him closer until he leaned his elbows on the grass at her side. He breathed in deeply and noticed she did the same, a fluttering pulse leaping to life at the junction of her neck and shoulder. Turning his head, he admired her openly, unable to tear his gaze away. She wore a bikini of brilliant blue that matched her eyes, like a little bit of the summer sky had fallen to earth. Her curves and dips and rounded places all called to him and he swallowed hard.

Her head lifted and their gazes met. A trace of fear shone in the depths and his wolf poked him in the nuts, insistent he take care of her.

"Do I frighten you?"

She licked her lips, leaving them wet and soft. He wanted to lean over to taste her so badly.

"I'm very drawn to you, and that scares me."

The air around them filled with the faint noises of the spring and the laughter of the others in the distance. The sunlight shone full on them and she turned her face to its warmth. He waited patiently. Patience was something he had more than enough of. It took a few minutes before she sat straighter, squaring her shoulders. The boldness with which she turned to face him made him proud. His mate was no wimp. He'd expect her to be as strong as him.

"I don't know how much my sister told you. I've been avoiding wolves for a long time. I know I need to change my reaction, but it's become a habit to stay away from any involvement with pack. I have to fight my first instinct. It's going to take time to retrain myself not to panic when I see a werewolf. I'm sorry I screamed when I saw you. You didn't deserve that."

She was not only strong, she was empathetic and caring. Erik let the pleasure of her presence roll over him. "Trust me, you're not the first person to scream at the sight of me. I'm a little larger than most people. That can be intimidating. I don't take it personally."

Maggie smiled. "Good for you."

They stared at each other.

"Would you be comfortable if I touched you?" she whispered, looking him straight in the eyes.

Comfortable? He was dying for her touch. "I'd love it."

She lowered her gaze again. "I haven't been around many wolves recently. I'm frightened by what I'm feeling. I think I know what this is, but I'm scared..."

Oh mercy. "I'll take care of you."

He took a step to the side, still standing waist deep in the water. With one hand on the grass on either side of her hips he caged her between his arms. They both glanced toward the others to make sure they weren't being watched. Then like conspirators, they leaned together and their lips connected.

Sweet summertime air. The feel of the wind through his

fur on a moonlight run. All the most treasured moments of his life faded in comparison as he tasted her. This, this was the moment he'd waited for all his life. She met him with her mouth slightly open, her breath mingling with his before their tongues even touched. He forced himself to keep his hands in place but she had no such compunction. As they kissed, slow and easy, learning each other's flavour, she caressed his shoulders, rubbing her palms over his brush cut. Smoothing her long fingers down his chest. His skin shivered in anticipation of where she would touch next. Light, fleeting touches that brought his blood to a boil.

He concentrated on enjoying her scent, drawing it into his very being. Nibbles on her bottom lip, light kisses across her cheek. He licked softly at the pounding pulse at her throat. His gums itched with the desire to bite, to mark her permanently as his. But not yet. Not now that she'd confessed her fears. Still, his wolf demanded he take some action. The beast within grew as wild as he'd ever felt it, driving Erik to claim his mate. Instead of biting he suckled, drawing the soft skin of her neck into his mouth until he'd brought the blood to stain the creamy surface. The moan of desire escaping her lips nearly made him change his mind and take her right there on the embankment.

Oh hell, he wanted her. All his. Now.

It took concentration to pull away, to watch her panting breaths slowly calm, his body aching for more. His gaze fell on the rosy circle marring her throat and his wolf grumbled with delight. *His mate.* He paused.

"Your friend is full human, isn't she?"

Maggie ran her hands over his shoulders again and again, her fingers clinging to him. She peeked at where Pam still played with the boys. "There's no way I can explain to her why I'd let a total stranger give me a hickey. She's going to think I've gone insane." She snorted. "Maybe I have. Oh Lord, I never expected this to happen."

Erik lifted her off the edge and lowered her into the water. He longed to pull her back onto his lap, and touch her more and more intimately. If this had been any normal situation, they would already be making love. It was the way with mates. Sometimes it took a lifetime to find the one special person who would complete you on every level—physical, mental and emotional. Once you found each other there was no hesitation. No recrimination for simply taking and joining together what was meant to be.

Waiting was going to kick his ass.

He took a seat on one of the underwater benches opposite her. "We don't have to tell her. She's flying back to Vancouver in a couple of days, right?"

Maggie nodded.

"We'll wait. As much as I want to take you back to my tent and make love with you right now, we can wait for the sake of your friend." A shiver shook Maggie briefly and she glanced at him, a trace of fear back in her eyes. His wolf howled and fought to comfort her. "What's wrong?"

"I don't want a mate."

He snorted. *Bullshit.* "Too bad. You've got one."

Her jaw dropped, and she gaped at him. "You can't just say something like that and expect me to be all right with it. I'm telling you I don't want a mate. I'm still freaked out at the thought of trying to live within the confines of a pack. Why would I also want a mate to deal with?"

That made no sense at all. "A mate isn't to deal with, a mate is to love."

She stopped cold. He had the sudden vision of the two of them, tangled together intimately, and had to reach into the water to adjust himself before his cock exploded. Her gaze followed his hands and she blushed hard.

"I know this isn't fair. I'm sorry, I really am, but as much as my body is interested, we can't do this. I'm telling you straight up so you can be prepared. Even after Pam leaves, I'm not having sex with you. I'm not ready to be anyone's mate until I deal with some issues."

"Are you telling me this because you think if you say it, you'll be able to resist wanting to be with me? Maggie, we're werewolves and we're mates. There's a chemical reaction between us, yes, but this isn't just physical. Becoming mates is in our best interest."

"Best interest? What the hell are you talking about?"

"Those issues you mentioned, let me help you with them. That's my job. As mates we're better as a couple. I need you, you need me."

"Arghh, you are so frustrating."

"I'm your mate."

The shouting and laughter from the others got louder as they moved closer. This conversation would have to be put on hold. Erik raised a brow at her. "We'll have to agree to disagree for now. Let's head back to the campground. We'll follow you to Whitehorse in the morning. Keil gave me orders to keep you in sight at all times while we're there." He stood and held out a hand to her. She took it reluctantly and he squeezed her fingers. "It's going to be okay, Maggie, really."

She shook her head. "You just don't understand."

They waded to the stairs and he led her out of the pool. "Maybe not, but that doesn't mean I don't care."

The bright hope in her eyes calmed his fears. There was obviously something big she wasn't sharing yet, but they'd deal with it. Together.

"Holy cow, what happened to your neck?" Pam exclaimed as she and the boys crowded around them.

Maggie froze for a second, her face flushing red. Erik stepped in smoothly. "Bug bite."

One of the boys snorted. Erik elbowed him in the ribs while Pam dug into her bag and pulled out a container of cream. She dabbed some on the mark. "Must have been a hell of a big bug."

Maggie glared at him and he smiled, turning away to head to the change room. "The biggest around."

3

"I've changed my mind about heading home. I'm canceling my flight, Maggie. I'm not letting you head off into the wilds of Alaska with this group of misfits." Pam folded her arms in front of her.

Maggie sighed. *Not again.* The entire seven-hour drive from Liard to Whitehorse, Maggie had struggled to answer her friend's endless, nosy questions.

It didn't help that during their couple days of sightseeing in Whitehorse before Pam's flight home, Erik shadowed them everywhere. He seemed to be trying his best to give them a little space but still refused to leave her alone.

"I'm not headed into the wild with them. I'm simply getting a ride to Haines to rejoin my family."

"Yeah, right. The family you've been soooo thrilled about. It's been years since your parents' accident. I thought you told me your sister was involved in some kind of a cult at one point. You never wanted anything to do with her friends when we were at university. There was that one time you even hid from them. Or don't you remember?"

A shiver ran over her skin at the memory. She wished she could forget. "Damn it, Pam. Of course I remember, but things have changed."

"*Riiiiiight.*"

Maggie hesitated. How was she supposed to convince Pam when she wasn't sure herself?

A wolf pack was supposed to be the safest place on earth. A place to be nurtured and cared for, not a hellish trap. That hadn't been her sister's experience, or her own. In defense, she'd rejected the pack of her youth, had even managed to reject the whole idea of being a wolf for a long period of her life. She couldn't do it anymore. Her body wouldn't let her.

But her heart and mind were terrified to take the next step.

She settled into one of the rigid plastic chairs in the airport waiting area. "Pam, I know it seems strange, but you've got to trust me on this. My sister and I have always kept in touch, and I love her dearly. Plus she's married to a wonderful guy now."

Pam shook her head reluctantly. "I just don't understand why after all this time you're deciding to move back to the Yukon. I thought we were going to keep rooming together. I'm...disappointed." She squatted beside Maggie. "I'm worried about your health. You've never shaken off this mono or whatever it is you've got. What if you have another attack while you're on the road?"

"That's part of the reason I won't be driving." She grabbed Pam's hands. "I'll be fine. Really. I'm so glad we got to spend this time together. You kick butt when it comes to singing on road trips." Pam snorted and they grinned at each other.

"I couldn't sing my way out of a paper bag." Suddenly

Maggie was wrapped in a huge hug, the breath squeezed from her body. Pam let her go only to shake a finger in her face. "I want regular emails. Let me know when you're settled, and if I don't hear from you often, I'm coming back with a gun."

Maggie laughed. "I expect you to visit me in Haines when you can. You've been an awesome friend, and I'm going to miss you."

One last final hug and Pam joined the short line winding its way through the security checkpoint.

Maggie felt him at her side before she saw him. While it freaked her out a little to have Erik hovering over her, it also felt very right. The two days while she'd shopped and visited the theater and museums with Pam, his presence in the background had reassured her. Made her feel safe. No wonder Pam thought she was crazy to go anywhere with him—he was like an obsessed stalker in her friend's eyes.

Now through final security, Pam turned back to wave farewell. She gave Erik a dirty look and held her fingers like a phone, pointing at Maggie and mouthing "call me".

Maggie would miss her, but dealing with the pack for the first time in years with a human around? Not a good idea.

"She's a nice girl." The deep timbre of his voice hit her low in the gut. "You okay?"

She nodded. The familiar protective layers she'd built around her for years were disappearing fast. Now she headed into dangerous territory. Was it possible to get comfortable being around a huge group of wolves again? Would she ever feel safe?

"I left the boys at the Canada Games Center to play for a while. I'd like to take my mate out for lunch." He slipped an arm around her, tugging her to his side.

A thrill shot through her at the layers of meaning she read into his words. His claim on her—she couldn't deny it was real. Her wolf pranced at the thought of going anywhere with him. Especially somewhere private where they could remove a few articles of clothing and get intimate.

She shook her head to break free of the images taunting her. She couldn't. They shouldn't. Not...yet. "I told you we're waiting. I meant it."

He twisted to face her, their bodies sliding closer. "You think it's too dangerous to share lunch with me?" Heat rolled off his skin, and she had to look way, way up to see into his eyes. Her mouth watered, her hormones kicking into high gear.

Bastard. He knew how much his touch affected her. "You're a royal pain in the ass."

"Not yet." He stroked her hip intimately, cupping her butt cheek in one palm briefly. He winked, then pressed his wide hand on her lower back to direct her steps toward the parking lot.

Heat shot through her core, and her wolf sat up and begged. Maggie jerked free from his touch by picking up the tempo. Of course, since her legs were much shorter, she almost had to run to outpace him.

Two rows farther into the parking lot she twirled and planted her hands on her hips. She needed to regroup before they headed to Haines.

"Look. I know you've got direct orders from your chief Pooh-Bah, but I'd like some time by myself. No one is going to accost me on the streets of Whitehorse. I'm perfectly safe. I used to live here. I just want to be left alone and..."

Lordy, how was she supposed to stay angry with him when every time she gave him hell, he did nothing but smile? It wasn't just any kind of smile, either. It was a do-you-want-to-crawl-into-bed-with-me-now kind of smile. The expression had a lot of impact when you placed it on his six-foot-five frame and added in his gorgeous features and his dark sparkling eyes.

Did he have to smell so damn good?

"You can't walk by yourself in Whitehorse. I don't know if you noticed over the past couple days, but there are a lot more wolves living here than in Vancouver. Not only are you a member of a rival pack, you're also related to a couple of the most powerful wolves in the North. Keil thought you were single. He didn't want any young pups trying to take advantage of you."

"I am single."

He growled softly, and her core muscles tightened in reaction. Oh shit, she'd pissed off his wolf. Icy fingers of dread raced up her spine, and her heart pounded. She wanted to drop to her knees and bare her throat in submission. Another part wanted to scramble away, to flee from his anger.

Somehow she kept her eyes open in the hopes she'd be able to duck if he swung at her. With his height advantage, he towered over her, and she felt overwhelmed by the sheer size of the man.

He lifted her chin with a single finger and spoke firmly. "You. Have. A. Mate."

Her wolf panted in agreement and crawled closer to the surface. She grabbed her stomach as cramping pain rocked her.

"Damn it, what the hell...?" Erik wrapped his arms around her, pulling her close.

Somehow she ended up in his lap as he squatted on his heels, his back against a rental car. The world spun in circles, and she scrambled for the vial of pills in her pocket. He took it from her, shook out a few and handed them over. From somewhere he produced a water bottle and she gulped greedily.

She kept her gaze averted. Between her fears and her rising need for him, she felt completely out of balance.

It didn't take long for the pain to ease. When she opened her eyes it was to stare into his concerned face.

"I'm so sorry. I didn't mean to scare you." He cupped her face in his big palm, examining her carefully.

She nodded slowly. All she sensed was his concern and desire. She ignored her tangled nerves and forced herself to calm down. He'd been nothing but trustworthy, and he deserved to be treated with respect.

"You want to tell me what's wrong?" he encouraged softly.

Maggie bit her lip. "Chemical imbalance." For now, that's all she wanted to admit.

He frowned. "You're a wolf. Change and you'll heal."

She scrambled off his lap and wavered for a second before his strong arm supported her. That was one topic she was nowhere ready to discuss. "I'm hungry. Can we have lunch?"

Erik eyed her as he led her to his SUV. "Nice try at changing the topic. Why are you fighting this so hard? You need—"

"I need lunch. Something raw. Is that possible here in Whitehorse?"

His smiled wryly. "I know just the place."

～

"A combo platter for four please."

Maggie elbowed him. "Four?"

Erik sniffed. She must be extra hungry, maybe that was part of her problem. Silly women were always on diets when they didn't need to be.

"Sorry, make it for six. Everything raw, extra wasabi on the side, and skip the pickled ginger." They grabbed spots at the end of the long counter and he held her high-backed stool as she sat, still chuckling.

"You turkey. That's not what I meant."

"What?" He captured her hand in his and held it. She might want to go slow, but there was no way he would let her completely ignore the fact they were meant to be together. He wanted to touch her, just to torment himself.

A flush covered her cheeks and she tugged slightly, testing his hold, before relaxing and squeezing his fingers.

"I'm sorry. I'm not making this easy for you." Her smile faded, and he hurried to reassure her.

"Trust me, I've seen mated pairs in action often enough to know their relationships are not always easy. I'm prepared for anything you send my way." He brushed the fingers of his free hand against her cheek. "I'm all yours."

The light chatter of tourists carried around them, the scents of people filled the air, but all he noticed was her. Bright blue eyes stared at him. The teasing light fragrance of her perfume, the stronger scent of her wolf—both filled his nostrils and clouded his mind.

His stomach rumbled and broke the intense connection between them. Concern for her health nagged at him. There was something wrong with his mate, and he struggled to understand. Wanted to fix things and make her better.

He needed more details. "You want to tell me what the pills are about?"

She wrinkled her nose. For a second he thought she

might try to lie, but then she sighed. "I've got some kind of chemical imbalance, and I discovered by chance the pills help change my blood pH enough to knock me back to normal levels for a while."

"I still don't see why your wolf doesn't heal you. Does Missy know about this?"

She nodded slowly.

That was good enough for now. For the past two years Missy had often shared her concern for her sister, how she felt Maggie needed to be back with family as soon as possible. He'd have more time to talk about the situation when they were safely in pack territory.

"I'll trust she'll do what she can to help you. You let me know if I can do anything, okay?" Erik kissed her cheek lightly, using the opportunity to suck in a deep breath of her scent.

Hell. This was sheer hell.

The area grew more crowded. Their tray of food arrived, distracting him for a second. Maggie stopped chatting, closing in on herself. Erik glanced around to see other wolves had joined them and now sat at the counter.

One slid closer to Maggie. "Hey, sweet thing. New in town?"

Erik lifted a brow. Was the man an idiot? Or blind?

It wasn't even worth making a commotion. Wordlessly, he transferred Maggie from her stool to his lap. He selected a piece of sushi and lifted it to her lips. "Ignore him. You said you were hungry. Try this."

She shot him a grateful look and snuggled closer. "Thank you, although you need to stop hauling me around like I'm a sack of potatoes."

She accepted the tidbit and her tongue stroked his skin.

He clenched his jaw hard to stop from growling out

loud. That's how she wanted to play it? Okay by him. Anything to keep touching her.

They might have been alone. The new wolves left quickly after realizing he and Maggie were together, and for the first time in a long while, Erik was glad his sheer size was enough to intimidate. Seated at the end of the restaurant counter, his back to the wall, Erik fed piece after piece of delicate salmon, fresh tuna and other sashimi to his mate.

After the first couple of times, Maggie shyly picked a portion and offered it to him in return.

He sucked her fingers into his mouth, licking them clean one by one, his gaze never wavering from hers.

She whimpered, soft and low in her throat, and he had to close his eyes to concentrate on keeping his wolf at bay. Everything about the woman called to him, and she seemed to be going out of her way to drive him wild. She was strong, but needed his protection. Smart, yet tender hearted. He drew her close and kissed her briefly, brushing their lips together. His hand skimmed over her thigh, tugging her closer into his lap and against his rising erection.

She had to know he wanted her.

Maggie licked her lips, then returned to feeding him.

It was as erotic as they could get in a public place. It was a good thing they *were* in a public place, or he'd never have lasted. A few of the barriers she'd raised between them seemed to have slipped away.

Erik glanced at his watch. There was just enough time to finish their meal, pick up the boys and be on their way. He chose another piece and held it to her lips.

He was going to enjoy every possible moment with his mate.

4

On the outskirts of Haines, Alaska, Erik turned down a long driveway. They passed a large log building Maggie assumed was the pack house. There was a meeting happening tonight, judging by the cars gathered three deep in the parking lot.

Another minute down the same road Erik pulled up in front of a tidy bungalow. An older home was tucked into the trees next to it.

He opened her door and helped her out, his fingers caressing hers lightly as he held her hand a little too long.

Why did he have to make her tingle?

Maggie shook her hand free and turned to admire her sister's home. This was far quieter and more up her alley than living in a common apartment like some packs did. Being with a mess of wolves right now? Ix-nay. Not something she could handle.

Being cooped up with Erik for the past four hours made her more than ready for a little space from him as well. He'd done nothing but chat quietly to her about the Granite Lake pack, and ask polite questions. After the sensuality of the lunch they'd shared, all that danced through her brain were visions of them naked.

It had been a very long four hours.

A tall, lean figure strode down the stairs to greet them. Spiky black hair and a wicked smile flashed for a second before he snatched her up and spun her in a circle.

"Welcome. It's about time you made it north to join us." Tad released her, ruffling her hair. She returned his grin and simply stood next to him, relaxing into the calm his presence cast over her. It was amazing how his skills as an Omega soothed her jangled nerves.

His brow shot upward and he hooted with laughter as he hugged them both. "Erik! You old dog. Congratulations, both of you."

Oh shit. Another side effect of being an Omega—she'd forgotten he'd sense right away the potential connection between her and Erik.

"Tad—"

"Missy is going to be so excited to know you're mates. This is fabulous news."

"Tad—"

"Erik, you coming in as well? Or will you come back to get her later?"

"Tad, *wait.*"

Finally he stopped to listen, his head cocked to the side. The sensation of a cool breeze floated from him, and she took a deep breath. The edge of her pain numbed as she took his hand.

Omega skills ran deep in both her sister and Tad, and she'd never been more grateful for a calming touch. She had to speak quickly before she lost her nerve. "Erik's not staying with me. Not yet."

Tad raised a brow, concern written on his face.

"Really?" He glanced between them for a few seconds before he shrugged. "Okay. Your choice. I guess we'll see you later."

Maggie turned to face the giant standing mere inches away. She kept her hands by her sides to stop from reaching for him and begging him to stay. "I..."

He tapped her lightly on the nose, his strong body and gorgeous features so tempting and reassuring at the same time. Love and concern poured from him. "I heard you. Right now, I'll give you space. Say hi to Missy for me, and I'll see you at dinner. You will sit with me."

She crossed her arms over her chest. *Bossy, arrogant...*

"Please." Erik winked at her, nodded at Tad, then strode across the deck toward the larger house on the adjacent property.

Maggie suddenly felt timid standing alone next to an Omega wolf—she wasn't scared of him, but he might be able to tell exactly what was wrong with her, and why. The reason for her attempt to return to the pack, as well as the reason she'd left in the first place.

Was she ready for anyone to know it all?

For many years she'd been on her own, dealing with her fears. She still wasn't ready to admit to anything more than she needed help healing her body. Maybe in a few weeks, or months, she could talk about the rest of the trouble. Now it was enough she was attempting to rejoin a pack on a trial basis.

She pasted on a bright smile before lifting her gaze to his. The expression on his face made her drop the façade. *Damn.*

"You know what's wrong with me, don't you? And why?"

He dragged a hand through his hair, staring into the

distance. When he looked back at her the anger and indignation she'd seen on his face were once again controlled.

He nodded slowly. "It's an Omega thing. Don't worry, I won't tell anyone, and I doubt Missy will pick it up. She's a little distracted right now. But, Maggie, you need to understand—you're safe here. Also, Erik is a rock. You can share anything with him."

Tad's simple statement, and the lack of pity in his eyes did more to ease her fears than anything else. "Thanks."

"Now, we'd better get inside. Missy's a trifle...touchy these days. I'm going out of my way not to piss her off."

The house was clean and tidy except for a few toys scattered around. Bright pictures and fabric filled the cozy rooms. Maggie admired what she saw as they moved at a quick pace through to the back of the house. There the kitchen faced the trees, and just to the side was a cheery sunroom with floor-to-ceiling windows. Missy sat curled up in one of the comfy chairs, basking in the sunlight.

"You're here!" Missy twisted in her chair and what Maggie thought was a pillow twisted with her. She threw her arms open wide, her eyes bright, and her smile from ear to ear. "I can't believe you're finally here. Come and give me a hug."

Maggie raced across the room, maneuvering as close as possible, wrapping her arms around her sister and relaxing into her embrace. The tears that had threatened earlier fell now as they held each other for the first time in what felt like forever.

Finally Missy patted her on the head and kissed her forehead. "I'm so glad to see you again."

The heavy bulge of Missy's baby-filled belly separating them moved, and Maggie pulled away in amazement.

"Oh my goodness, you're..." *Oops*. Gigantic was probably not a good thing to say to a pregnant woman.

"Huge? Damn it, I don't feel like a wolf, I feel like a beached whale."

Maggie laughed. "There's never been more of you to love than now."

"Oh gee, good one. Like I've never heard that before."

They grinned at each other and the years apart faded away. Missy was family—all the family she had left—and Maggie desperately needed family right now.

She reached out to give Missy's hand one more squeeze. "Thanks for letting me join you."

"You're going to be working for your keep, trust me. I can't move fast enough to keep up with Jamie. I'm so glad he won't be able to shift into a wolf until he's a teenager. He's hard enough to catch at eighteen months."

Maggie glanced around the room, looking for her nephew. "Where is he?"

"Sleeping. I think. I don't hear rockets going off, so he must still be locked in his room."

Tad dropped a kiss on his mate's forehead before squatting beside her.

Missy glared at him. "Finally. Did you get me—?"

He thrust out a handful of brightly coloured chocolate bars. "Dark chocolate. Plus orange chocolate...with walnuts."

Missy stared, disgruntled, her mouth twisting. She planted both hands on the sides of her chair to heave herself into a new position.

Tad rushed to help her.

She smiled sweetly at him and started again. "After you left, I decided I also wanted—"

"—dried smoked salmon. There's one bag on the table. I left the rest in the fridge."

Maggie laughed behind her hand. "Missy, are you trying to be difficult?"

Her sister pouted. "It's his damn fault I'm a bloated beach ball. Again."

Tad winked. "All my fault. I confess." Maggie watched in amusement as the two of them teased and verbally sparred for a minute before he rose, kissing Missy's cheek once again. "I'm going to leave you two ladies alone to get reacquainted. I'll take Jamie with me, but we'll be back in time to escort you to dinner."

"I want pickles at dinner."

Maggie burst out laughing as Tad shook his head slowly. "You hate pickles."

"I want them."

Tad snickered at Maggie. "Pickles. At least it's not pickles and ice cream. That would be too cliché."

"Your fault," Missy restated.

He blew her a kiss. "I seem to remember you were there too."

He ducked the pillow she threw and left.

The sun shining in made the room a warm haven of peace. To the side of the open window, an indoor water feature splashed and tinkled, the sound calming and reassuring. Missy adjusted herself, stretching her legs in front of her.

Maggie stared in amazement at the perfectly round protrusion extending from her sister's stomach. "You really are a beach ball."

"Shut up. Wait until you meet your mate and get pregnant. You're not much taller than me. There's nowhere for the baby to go but out, and this time with two of them..." Missy paused, then narrowed her eyes. Maggie felt her face heat up. "Holy moly, you've met your mate. Haven't you?"

Maggie leaned back in her chair and crossed her arms. "Anyone ever tell you it's damn hard to have a conversation with you when you seem to know everything, about everybody, before they tell you? It was bad enough when we were young, but since you've accepted you're an Omega, it's gotten ridiculous."

Missy snorted. "It's worse than you think. With Tad being an Omega too, we occasionally have really freaky conversations. Quit stalling. Who is it?"

Maggie stared out the window. "I'm not ready for a mate."

"Who is it?" Missy rubbed her hands with glee. "Someone in Vancouver? Why didn't he come with you? Is he making arrangements to move north, too?"

Maggie stood and wandered away a few steps. She didn't need this. Not now. Did Missy not realize how difficult it was to be surrounded by wolves again for the first time in years? Had she forgotten what it was like to be truly afraid?

The only reason Maggie had maintained any contact with their old pack was to keep in touch with Missy. As soon as Missy had mated with Tad, Maggie instantly severed all final ties with Whistler.

Her sister wouldn't drop the topic. "You met him in Whitehorse? Mags, you do realize this might be the solution to your problem."

Yeah, right. "Listen to me? I don't want to be tied to a mate. I'm still wondering if I made the right decision to come and be with your pack." She looked down at her sister. "How can you be so comfortable around all these wolves?

After everything they did to you? All those years of your life wasted because our Alpha—"

"Oh, honey, I've told you this so many times over the past two years. *These* wolves have been nothing but kind to me. Our Alpha wasn't an Alpha—not in the truest sense of the word. Tad is more than twice the man my first husband ever was. I'm happy now, Mags, really I am. Yeah, it was a rotten situation, and I didn't deserve to be treated like that, but I've moved on. Isn't it time you did the same?"

The only person in the world Maggie knew who had gone through more hell than she had sat before her, huge with her second and third children. Living with a man she trusted, who went out of his way to make her smile.

Was it really possible to leave the past behind?

"Maggie. Tell me. Please."

It was impossible to resist her.

"Erik." Maggie squeezed her eyes tight as her body reacted to even saying his name.

Her wolf woke again, this time with a slow and sensuous stretch itching up her spine. She hadn't felt that sensation in years.

Complete and utter silence greeted her announcement. She poked open an eye to see Missy sitting with her mouth gaping open. "What?"

Missy giggled naughtily. "You don't want to know."

"Bullshit. You made me tell you who it is, now spill. Do you not trust him?"

Her sister gasped. "Not trust Erik? The Friendly Giant? Girl, there is no one I trust more, except Tad and my Alpha. I was just imagining...umm...the two of you together. That's all."

Oh God. Not what she needed right now. "Great. I tell you I found my mate, and the first thing that jumps to your mind is how we're going to manage sex. You're such a bitch."

They both laughed. "Yeah, well, sex is kinda up there on my 'things to think about' list these days since I'm not getting much."

Maggie rolled her eyes. "Enough. I haven't accepted the mating yet. I need to figure other things out first."

Missy lifted her belly with her hands and wiggled to the front of her chair. "What you're not taking into consideration is with Erik as your mate, he'll help you figure those *things* out. You need help, and he's the one able to give it. You need to trust him."

"Stop being a bloody oracle."

"I'm not being an oracle, I'm being an Omega. More importantly, I'm being your sister and I only want the best for you. Why are you fighting so hard? Erik is a good man, and he's gorgeous. If I wasn't mated I'd be interested in a roll in the hay with him."

A low growl burst from Maggie. She froze in shock.

"Oops, looks like your wolf isn't as asleep as you thought."

Maggie dropped back into the chair opposite her sister. "No, she's getting more and more vocal, especially when it comes to Erik."

"That's a good thing."

The delight in her sister's eyes bothered her. *Get a mate, solve all your problems.* Maybe it just wasn't that easy. Maggie jerked to a standing position.

"So you say, but I'm not convinced. I only met him a few days ago. I need more time." She scrubbed her hands over her face, rubbing her temples. Her body and mind ached. Plus she wanted Erik so badly she could scream, but she was attempting to ignore those sensations. "I'm tired.

I'm hoping to catch up on my sleep tonight before I hop into nanny mode for you."

Missy wrinkled her nose. "Heading to bed? Already? But we have plans."

Oh hell, no. "I can't do any big events yet. I only have to see you and Tad, right? At least for a while?"

Missy hemmed and hawed a few times. Something was up. "Dinner has been planned. The Alphas will be there. You can't insult Keil and Robyn and not come."

Shit. Her first night here, and already she felt like running into the woods and hiding. She gritted her teeth and spoke through tight lips. "Fine."

"There's the Alpha's brother, TJ. And...well..."

"Erik's going to be there, isn't he?"

"He goes where the Alpha goes, especially formal events."

The only sound was the water tinkling in the fountain. Maggie turned to stare in horror at her older sister. "*Formal* events? What are you talking about?"

Missy sighed. "I'm really sorry, Mags, I didn't do it on purpose. There's kind of this thing tonight. It's a big deal around the wolf community and it only happens every five years. I didn't realize the timing overlapped when you called to say you were arriving. I don't know if you remember from when we lived in Whitehorse before moving to Whistler. The AWG?"

"The Arctic Wolf Games? Those are now?"

"Yeah. The selection banquet for the Granite Lack pack is tonight. That's why there's a crowd of cars at the pack house." Panic must have shown on her face because Missy rushed to reassure her. "Honey, it's going to be okay. I'll sit with you, and Tad will, and we can leave as soon as they finish the announcements."

A shiver of fear rolled over Maggie. There was going to be a gathering of wolves and she had to go.

Welcome to hell.

~

SHE KEPT her back against the wall for as long as possible. Hidden in the shadows, she watched the pack members stroll around the large hall, chatting and laughing.

It looked safe. For now.

"You okay?"

She bit back a little scream. "How did you sneak up on me like that?"

Erik stroked a finger down her arm, his eyes sparkling with mischief. "I've been here for five minutes watching you. I thought you might like an escort back to the table. We're going to do the selection soon, and it'll get a little noisy in here."

She swallowed hard. Somehow her fingers snuck their way into his. The warmth of his hand reassured her, calming her slightly. There were a hell of a lot more wolves in the building than she had ever wanted to see in her life again. Still, she couldn't hide in the corner all night, no matter how much she wanted to.

"Okay." She stood straighter and held her head high. She might be shaking inside, but there was no way she would let any of the pack know.

Erik squeezed her fingers as he led her past the Alpha and his mate. The two of them smiled at her before turning their attention back to the man seated beside them.

"They like you." Erik pulled out her chair, next to Missy. He sat on her other side and draped his arm along the backrest.

The curls of hair on his arm tickled the back of her neck and her nipples tightened. Great. She was freaking out with fear *and* getting aroused.

His mouth was next to her ear. "I like you too. Very much." He licked her earlobe.

A shockwave raced through her system. *Shit.* "Stop that."

His soft voice tickled her. "I can smell your desire."

She elbowed him, and he moved away slightly, chuckling.

Missy leaned over. "You okay? We can go now if you want. Seriously, we've put in our appearance, we can leave."

Maggie shook her head violently. She just wanted to get to the end of the bloody evening so she could curl up in a ball and collapse, but she refused to appear weak.

At the head table an older man in a business suit rose, the badge on his suit jacket marked with the initials AWG. He cleared his throat and the room hushed.

"The Arctic Wolf Games will begin three days from now in Skagway, Alaska. The rest of the teams have already been selected, and are en route to the first challenge. The captain of the four-wolf team from Granite Lake will be selected first from a pool of ten hopefuls submitted by your Alpha. The other three will be filled by random selection. As always, the events involve both physical and mental abilities, so strength and speed are not the only abilities honoured.

"Every pack member over twenty is eligible. Your Alpha has already removed the names of those members who for one reason or another aren't capable of taking part in the Games. Like your Omega, obviously."

"Yeah, cause she'd kick their butts," some wiseass in the back shouted, and the room rang with laughter.

Maggie wrapped her arms around herself to keep her limbs from shaking. It was too noisy, too many bodies and just too much. She glanced to her right, her fingers itching to re-grasp Erik's hand.

He returned her gaze, reaching to clasp her fingers and anchor her spinning world.

The chairman dug into the bag and pulled out a paper, holding it aloft. With great pomp he opened it and leaned into the microphone. "The first competitor, and team captain for Granite Lake, is—Erik Costanov."

Roars of delight filled the hall. Erik squeezed her fingers for a second before releasing them to stand and wave at the pack members who all cheered and clapped.

"Damn straight. Finally we'll have a chance at winning this thing."

Maggie looked at her sister in confusion.

"Granite Lake has never won. They've never even placed. The random-lottery method of selecting the team means most years there's been a team or two with a ringer. It looks like this time it's our turn. This is fantastic."

Something went cold in Maggie's soul. She might not be ready to take Erik as her mate, but selfishly she wanted him nearby. "Will he be gone for long?"

Missy shook her head. "The Games themselves take about ten days. You can always go along as a spectator." She smiled and touched Maggie's arm softly. "Are you thinking you'll miss him? That's a good sign."

Maggie shuddered. "I'm not going to hang out with more than a hundred wolves for a week. Tonight is bad enough, and it's only bearable because you're here."

"And Erik. Be honest."

Damn it anyway. Sisters were a pain in the butt. "Fine. It's easier when he's next to me."

Conversations filled the hall for a while as Erik chatted with the selection chairman. He smiled across the room at her like she was the only thing he cared about.

Maybe...this would work out. Eventually. She knew better now than to deny her wolf, and the urge to get together with Erik grew stronger by the minute.

If only she didn't feel like vomiting from simply looking out over the sea of bodies in the hall.

The chairman repeated his routine, selecting another name from a larger bag this time. With a loud yell, a man somewhere in his late twenties threw himself into the air, clasping his hands over his head and shaking them in victory. He strolled forward, taking the time to stop and plant a kiss on a pretty girl near the front of the hall.

Missy leaned in again and whispered with a laugh. "Oh goodie, that's Jared Gilliland. If there's a challenge involving getting into the girls' pants, we're now guaranteed a win."

Rather than watching what happened with the selection, Maggie was more intent on keeping an eye on Erik. He shook his new team member's hand then stood back, his gaze once again meeting hers. Calming her from across the room.

He was there for her. Could she believe that? She'd been taught all her life her wolf was an important part of her, not something she could deny. She'd challenged that teaching to her own detriment.

Maybe Missy's lovingly delivered lectures over the past two years had been right. Maybe it was time to move on.

Lost in thought she barely heard the chairman call the next name.

"Margaret Raynor."

Terror raised its head and choked her throat closed. "I can't..."

Her voice was a ghost of a whisper. Confused questions rang throughout the room.

"Margaret who?"

"Is she really eligible?"

The Alpha stood and raised a hand. The chaos stilled as Keil looked out over the room. "She is eligible. Maggie officially joined the pack two years ago when her sister became Omega for Granite Lake. I have no troubles with her appointment to represent our pack."

Keil's gaze stayed steady on her. His smile did little to calm the butterflies doing backflips in her belly. She didn't like attention from an Alpha, no matter what her sister said about the man.

The pack quieted at Keil's words, and everyone resumed eating and chatting. She couldn't do this. She'd ruin everything for the whole lot of them, and the Games were a big deal.

More than a few curious glances were thrown her way as she excused herself and made her way over to Erik. "I need to talk to you."

The pleasure in his eyes at her request hurt. She didn't want to be the one to ruin what should be a special day. She tugged him back into the corner of the hall. He knelt by her side so their heads were closer to level.

Oh shit, was she really going to tell him? She had to. She grabbed him by the collar and put her lips inches from his ear to make her confession.

"I can't shift."

He'd wrapped his arms around her without her even noticing. Now his hands tightened where they held her waist. "What?"

She fought to get it out before she lost her courage and simply ran from the confining and overwhelming setting of the hall. "Some of the challenges are done in wolf form, right? I can't shift. I haven't for over seven years."

Erik stared for a moment before folding her closer, their bodies touching.

"Thank you for telling me." He kissed her forehead gently. "Don't worry about it."

Maggie gaped at him. "But...did you *hear* me? I can't shift. We'll automatically lose any challenge requiring us all to be wolves. I don't need a group of wolves pissed off at me. I need to decline, or whatever."

He shook his head. "You can't decline. If you step down, we compete with three. No substitutes are allowed. As for the rest, you need to trust me. Remember the mate thing? We're a couple, and there's no challenge we can't face together."

His totally honest and straightforward answer did something to the block of ice enclosing her heart. Maggie reached out and latched onto his collar again, dragging their lips together.

Instant need. Passion and desire rocked her body. Moreover, she felt safe. Loved. His fingers tangled in her hair as he angled her mouth to the side, his tongue stroking her lips, her teeth, the roof of her mouth. They wrapped around each other in the corner of the hall, and she was oblivious to anything but the raging fire sweeping over her.

A roar rose from the crowd. A mixture of laughter, jeers and moans.

Maggie jerked to attention and squirmed back. The sound, so overwhelming and loud, frightened her, and she clung to his forearms even as Erik released her. He cupped her cheek for a moment before leading her back to the head table, keeping her safely tucked under his arm. "What's the fuss?"

The chairman sniffed. "Didn't you hear the selection for the final member of your team?"

Erik glanced down at Maggie and grinned. "Nope. I was kind of distracted."

A long-limbed young man sauntered forward. Maggie frowned. He looked barely old enough to take part in the Games, although the resemblance to the pack Alpha was uncanny. So this was the younger brother she'd been told about.

"TJ?"

The gangly male flashed them double thumbs-up. "Hey, big guy. Let's win this thing!" He reached to give Erik a high five, and tripped over his own feet.

5

The wind picked up as they left the natural harbor of Haines behind, cruising on the forty-five minute ferry ride to Skagway. Erik leaned on the railing and watched Maggie out of the corner of his eye. She sat by herself, away from where the rest of the group traveling to the Games lounged, laughing and goofing off.

He'd been busy the past two days. Not so busy he couldn't have made time for her. Hell, all he wanted to do was spend time with her, but she'd asked for space to prepare herself for the contest. He'd given it to her.

Now he wondered if it had been the right choice. The sweet kisses she'd bestowed on him had revved his motor and made him long for her to join him full-time—in his bed and in his life. Now she stayed back. Separating herself from him and holding to her fear like a coat of armor.

Funny how quickly his perspective changed. Until last week the most important thing in his life had been his position as Beta to the pack, and his friendships with Keil and Tad. His job? It had always been an extension of being there for people. He'd long ago dealt with his demons and life had been floating along just fine.

Until Maggie.

For a small package she was a bundle of trouble. She ran hot and then cold, and both sides drove him nuts. Not only did the mate connection draw him to her, but he was used to protecting the weak.

When she looked around, like she did now, with fear filling her pretty blue eyes, he could barely hold himself back from grabbing her and attempting to erase all her sadness.

Then she'd flip and get all tough and powerful, and that side was mighty attractive too. Both of them were strong wolves, and the temptation to see how strong she could be teased him.

Sex between them was going to rock, if they could get past her freezing up every time he walked near.

The pack members wandered down the deck, leaving a clear path between Maggie and him. Pleasure filled him as she rose and made her way across the space, seeking him out. He opened his jacket to offer her protection from the wind. She wavered, her eyes dilating as she licked her lips.

His body hardened.

She stepped back a pace and shook her head. "Don't do that. Not now. I'm barely managing to hold it together."

He shrugged. "Just thought I could warm you a bit."

She stuck her hands in her pockets and stared up at the sky. "We need to talk about this whole situation. How are we supposed to deal with the contests? I can't shift, and I don't really want to be around all these wolves."

"It won't be as bad when we start the competition. Usually they have staggered starts for events, depending on what they are. You'll have only myself, Jared and TJ around."

She lowered her head and he caught his breath. The blue orbs were filled with tears. "I don't want to do this. Not any of it. I wish I could just go home."

Screw being patient. Erik stepped forward and gathered her in his arms. He held her, rubbing her back and trying to get the tight knots in her shoulders to relax. Whatever burden she carried was driving him crazy.

"I know you don't want me to say this, but sweetheart, you are home."

Maggie pushed herself away until she could look into his eyes. "I'm scared."

"I see that. But you're also very strong. You're also not alone. I'll do what I can to help you. Unfortunately, whatever it is you fear, we'll have to deal with eventually. The issue of your wolf, I'll worry about. Trust me."

"Trust you? Right." She paced away, her arms folded over her chest. She glared at him. "This mate thing really sucks, you know? Because as much as I want to just go hide, I can't help but want to be with you and it's part of what scares me."

Erik frowned. "Why would being with me scare you?"

Maggie hesitated.

Ah shit. "Is it because I'm so big?"

She dropped her gaze.

Great. Another instance of being judged at first glance. He hadn't expected it from his mate and it hurt more than he thought it would. He turned away to face the water. The demons were buried deep, but obviously not as completely gone as he'd imagined. Her opinion mattered a great deal.

A soft touch on his sleeve caught his attention. He looked down into her gentle face. "It's not your size. To tell the truth, I'm kinda...attracted to how big you are." She blushed and he coughed lightly. *Oh yeah.* She rushed on. "What I'm scared about is you going all wolfie on me and being overprotective. I don't need it. I can take care of myself."

He shrugged. "I won't go all he-man on you."

"Oh yeah? You can control the wolf so well you won't hurt anyone who touches me?" She walked away from him, leaning her back on the sidewall of the passenger compartment.

This conversation grew more confusing by the second. "What are you talking about?"

"I saw it. In the Whistler pack, there was an incident. Tell me it wouldn't infuriate you if I...hugged someone. Or kissed them."

Holy shit. Missy had told them a few stories about her time in her old pack, but there were obviously more issues than he'd been aware of.

He crossed to her side and knelt to take her hands in his, warming them between his palms. "I wouldn't like it, but I can behave responsibly. I don't think my reaction would be any wilder than a typical human man. I do have control. I've worked hard at it."

"Really?"

He nodded. "Really. Being the biggest guy around means there's always someone who wants to prove how tough they are by taking me on. I don't agree with violence as a first resort."

She stared at him for a long time, a curious expression in her eyes. A crowd of noisy tourists poured onto the deck, and her gaze narrowed, her face growing red.

What was going on in her devious mind?

Maggie walked slowly toward the crowd, glancing over

her shoulder as if making sure he watched. She tapped one of the young men in the group on the shoulder and smiled sweetly at him before saying something. The man shrugged.

She looked over her shoulder again, then grabbed the stranger. The whole group started talking loudly as she planted a huge kiss on his lips before releasing him and strolling back to where Erik stood.

He checked his blood pressure. He checked his temper. Both seemed normal, and the taunting look in her eyes did nothing but fill him with amusement. Okay, that was interesting. His wolf even snickered a little, seeing the humor in what she'd attempted to do.

Contentment rolled over him. He really did have this under control.

Now he just had to deal with her underestimating him.

He lifted her chin with his finger so their eyes could meet. "Just what do you think that proved?" She chewed on her lower lip, a crease marring the space between her eyes. Ahh, he hadn't reacted as she'd expected. "Should I go hit him? Fine."

"Erik, wait. I'm..." She grasped his hand. He patted her fingers gently before letting her hand fall away. He wandered over to the confused gathering, his amusement growing by the second.

The men were speaking Russian, and he understood their words with ease.

"What was that all about, Dmitri?"

"I don't know, but I think I like American girls."

Erik held out his hand and spoke to them in their own language. "Hello. My name is Erik Costanov. I'm sorry, my wife was teasing you. Are you enjoying your holiday in Alaska?"

He chatted with them for a while, the young men

telling about the sights they'd seen on their cruise through the Inside Passage. He gave them a few recommendations for restaurants to try in Skagway and Anchorage. With enthusiastic pats on the back and lots of laughter, Erik said goodbye and returned to where Maggie sat on the stairs.

She wiggled her nose and scooted over to make room for him beside her. They sat silently for a while before she turned her red flushed face toward him.

"I didn't know you could speak Russian."

"There are a lot of things you don't know about me." Her scent rose and tickled his nose, and he took a deep breath, storing it for later. He could hardly wait to be able to sleep with her in his arms.

She spoke softly. "You just don't look like the type."

"Appearances can be deceiving. For example, you don't look like the type to get jealous easily, but I bet if I did what you just did, your wolf wouldn't like it very much."

She jerked upright and a faint growl escaped from her lips.

Hmm, his suspicions were correct. Her wolf was there, just hiding. He'd have to think about how he could convince her to trust him so they could lure the creature back to the surface. After seven years, this could get rough.

Maggie nodded deliberately then a mischievous expression crossed her face. "Well maybe, maybe not. Tell you what, you go ahead and kiss that guy, and we'll see what happens."

He laughed along with her. It was enough of a win for this time. Another of her defenses had fallen away, and when she leaned willingly into his side, his world grew a little warmer.

∼

MAGGIE PICKED up the pack and fiddled with the straps, adjusting them again. There was nothing wrong with the backpack. The whole situation gave her the heebie-jeebies.

"Are you nearly ready to go?"

She squealed and dropped the pack. How in the hell he managed to sneak up on her when he was so huge, Maggie could not understand.

She nodded, grabbing at his hand to stop him from turning away. "I'm worried about passing out. What if I have a reaction while I'm on the hike and—"

"There are medical crews providing help if anyone gets hurt. This isn't a war where we expect you to die in the field." He rubbed a circle on her palm with his thumb, and a flash of heat ran up her spine. "You haven't had any troubles since the night of the banquet, have you?"

Maggie thought for a minute. He was right. Her last dizzy spell had been back in Whitehorse. The last couple of days while she'd been at her sister's, getting ready for the Games, she'd felt fine. The most energized and healthy she'd been for years.

"I feel..." The expression in his eyes sucked the truth from her lips. "I feel great."

He winked at her. "Wonder if it has something to do with being with other wolves. Like your sister suggested?"

Oh shit, no way. She looked around his bulk at the other teams standing in groups, waiting to begin the first event. The teams from Whitehorse and Denmark were already underway. The Tombstone pack stood at the line ready for their turn in the staggered start.

"I just don't want to make trouble for the team. I've brought my pills along in case, but I'm not going to be able to do this hike very quickly. I hope I don't disappoint you."

He crossed his arms for a moment, leaning his torso

away from her. It was impossible to not admire the bulk of his arms, his biceps bulging his T-shirt. "It's not a race for speed. We have to solve puzzles as we go along. I expect you'll keep up just fine, and you're going to be a big help in contributing to us winning this event."

He spoke with such confidence her fears faded a little.

Erik motioned to the others. "Come on, team, let's take another look at the instructions. We have thirty minutes still until our start."

They gathered around, backs to the trees at the edge of the clearing. Before them the Dyea flats stretched to meet the ocean. The early-afternoon air was warm with the promise of heating up nicely in a few hours.

Erik spread out the map at their feet and traced the route they would follow. She was happy to see that once they started hiking, they'd be in the trees for the first third of the hike.

"Three days is the maximum time allotted to complete the thirty-three miles to Bennett Lake. That's a good solid hike, not a sprint pace. We'll be going faster than the original Gold Rushers, but we don't have to carry as much gear. However, we not only have to reach the checkpoint in time, we have a series of clues to find. Some of them will be used later in the Games challenges."

"What if we can't find them all?" TJ asked.

"Missing one or two, we have a chance. Missing more will make the final challenge tough to win. So this isn't a sprint. We'll camp out for two nights, and I really don't care if we see other teams passing us." He winked at Maggie. "It's not a *race*, although some of the other teams will try to convince you it is. This is a setup for later events. All we have to do is finish."

He pulled out the puzzle instructions, spreading them

on the ground next to the map. Jared leaned a little too close, and Maggie drew away, backing into the safety of Erik's side.

He casually shifted his position, tucking her against his body and she relaxed. Why did he have to feel so good?

She looked down at the strange maps. Contour lines, altitude markers, not much else. "They're not giving GPS waypoints, are they?"

He shook his head. "We have to do this the old-fashioned way with only compasses and our noses. For this challenge, one of the team travels in wolf. They can shift back at night, but while on the trail and searching for clues, they have to be in their animal form."

Maggie's throat closed tight and she found it hard to breathe. One of them was going to turn into a wolf. She had to be around a wolf.

She was going to die.

Without saying a word, Erik rubbed her back, a slow, soothing motion. She closed her eyes and concentrated on the feel of his hand instead of the gnawing fear in her belly.

TJ cursed as his foot caught the edge of the paper and it ripped. "Damn it, sorry. Look, I'd like to volunteer to be the one who stays in wolf." He wrapped his long arms around his legs as trying to avoid touching anything near him. "I know I've got a bad rep, but I am capable of pulling my own weight, especially if you keep me in my wolf form for most of the Games. It's just my human form that sucks rocks when it comes to coordination."

For the first time Maggie examined him more closely. He was as dark as his brother, the Alpha, but nowhere near as bulky. Long limbs, square jaw. TJ was a pretty good-looking fellow, he just never seemed to be in the right place at the right time. There was a dark-coloured stain on his shirt where she'd seen someone bump into him and dump their ketchup-covered fries all over.

Erik nodded. "I hoped you'd volunteer for the position, but not because I plan to keep you in wolf the whole time. You have an awesome sense of smell, and we need it for this challenge." TJ grinned, his limbs jerking in enthusiasm. Erik pulled the map out of range in the nick of time and laughed. "You're getting better. You've still got a little growing up to do, that's all."

The pleased expression in TJ's eyes made Maggie forget some of her own fears. Over the past couple of days, every other time someone mentioned TJ's name, he had been called a klutz, whether he was standing there or not.

Suddenly she felt indignant for him. What kind of crap was that?

"You just don't want to carry a pack." Jared poked TJ in the side and the two of them fell to the ground to wrestle like puppies for a minute.

A tug on her sleeve caught her attention and she followed Erik off to the side a few steps.

"I'm going to get TJ to change now. You okay?"

How did he know? "I...have to be, don't I?"

He stepped closer and spoke softly, for her ears only. "You think I haven't noticed you've tensed every time one of the other teams had a member shift? I didn't think it was because you were embarrassed by their nudity."

"Well, there was that one guy..."

"Hush." He kissed her nose, and she went all soft and melty inside. Three days on the trail with him. It was going to be heaven and hell.

Oh no, they would be camping out. How was she supposed to avoid him in the evening? Avoid giving in to the attraction between them that grew by the minute? It was one thing to say she wanted to hold off on becoming mates, it was another to stick to her guns.

TJ stripped off his clothes and folded them neatly, slipping everything into one of the three packs waiting nearby. Maggie admired his muscular body. He might have two left feet in human form, but it was a pretty nice package of clumsy altogether.

A low grumble from her left distracted her and she turned to see Erik staring, one brow raised. "Have you seen enough? Or do you want him to pirouette?"

No way. "Are you jealous?"

"Yes." The warmth he'd started earlier grew into raging heat. "I want you to look at me like that, not at TJ. I want to see admiration in your eyes for *me*—for your mate. It doesn't mean I'm going to go Rambo on his ass, but I'd appreciate if you'd stop drooling in front of me."

Maggie stepped into his body space and wrapped her arms around his torso, hugging him as close as she could.

"I'm sorry. I didn't mean to hurt you." Her instant need to comfort him puzzled her. Being in his arms satisfied something deep inside. Made her wolf rumble, low and needy.

He stroked one hand down her back, the fingers of his other hand running though her hair. He held her for a minute, their heartbeats slowly synchronizing, and it felt so damn good she almost forgot where they were.

"It's okay. Apology accepted. He's a good-looking kid, and an even better-looking wolf. You ready to meet him?"

She froze. TJ had shifted. Had Erik deliberately distracted her?

Knotting her fingers in his shirt, she glanced over her shoulder. TJ sat on his haunches, his tongue lolling to the side as he panted in the heat of the noontime sun. His silver-grey fur shone, his eyes were bright and his nose twitched as he sniffed the air.

She reminded herself again—it was TJ. They were in public. Erik was nearby. "He is a goo...good...looking wolf...isn't he?"

She could do this. Only she wasn't doing it alone. She grabbed Erik, tugging him with her as she approached. She held out her hand, palm open like a person would with a strange dog.

"What the hell?" Jared muttered.

"Let her be," Erik ordered. He squatted to the side and ran his free hand over TJ's flank. Maggie had to be squeezing the blood out of his other hand.

TJ tilted his head to the side, confused, before sniffing her palm. His wet nose brushed her skin and goose bumps rose all over her body. He licked her fingers, then plopped on his belly at her feet.

And rolled over.

Her wolf howled with delight, fighting to take control, fighting to break free. A wave of dizziness rushed her.

Erik's grip tightened and he moved to support her. "Okay?"

Wilderness. Starlit skies. Cool mountain water. The wind in her fur. Maggie ached for all the things she'd missed for so long. Again her wolf bumped the surface, making her blood sing, making the knot in her belly loosen a little more.

She shook off Erik's supporting arms and reached for TJ, touching his chest, running her fingers along the stiffer fur of his muzzle. She took a deep breath and soaked in the scent of a wolf giving her obeisance. It felt good. Oh so very good.

"Granite Lake. You're up in ten minutes. You can take

your place at the starting line." The Games Marshal passed them quietly, headed back to the officials' area.

TJ scrambled to his paws. Erik smiled at her as he helped her up. He kept hold of her hands. "Are we ready?"

He wasn't talking about the event. Maggie squared her shoulders and let the joy inside her shine out a little as she nodded.

For the first time in years she felt like there really was hope.

6

———

$\mathcal{M}$aggie drew another deep breath of crisp mountain air into her lungs before quick-stepping to catch up. Erik walked ahead of them with TJ. She found herself surprised to be enjoying the chance to get to know Jared better.

"You've lived in the North long?"

Jared scrambled over a fallen log blocking the trail then turned back to give her a hand. The trail was in good shape, except for people with short legs.

"All my life. I've always been in the Granite Lake pack too. I tell you, things have really changed in the past couple of years. Since Keil and Erik took over running things, conditions have improved so much."

He lowered her to the ground then motioned for her to walk ahead of him.

"What do you mean *improved*?"

"The old Alpha and his crew, they never cared about stuff like the Games. Too far beneath them. It's not just special events like this one. Man, at times it's tough getting a job in Haines, but Erik and Keil have things arranged so there is never a chance for any of the pack to be unemployed." He laughed. "That doesn't mean you won't be working your ass off. They seem to be able to find the dirtiest, rottenest jobs around for the pack members who are slow to get their acts together. No, it's been good to see the younger kids find a way to stay in the North instead of having to head south where their wolves aren't as happy. Plus the old timers? You see them regularly around the pack house now, where before they used to hide out since no one wanted to listen to them talk. Especially the real old geezers who forget they've told the same tale a million times."

She stopped to take a drink from her water bottle, thinking for a moment. It didn't sound like huge changes to her. Well, jobs were good, but she'd been thinking in the line of murder and other crimes being the issues, not laziness and neglect. "Did you know Erik spoke Russian?"

"Of course. He knows seven languages."

She jerked the bottle from her lips, the water sloshing down the front of her shirt. "*Seven?*"

Jared leaned back on a nearby tree, looking at her with a curious expression on his face.

"What?" she demanded.

"You're very pretty."

She felt heat race over her skin. The admiration in his eyes embarrassed her, and inside her wolf sniffed with disdain. "Thank you."

"Is there something between you and Erik? TJ swears you two are scented like mates, but..." He shrugged. "You're not acting like it. Just in case you're interested in a—"

"I don't want to get involved with you." Maggie's tongue tripped over itself in her hurry to turn him down. An icky sensation covered her at the thought of touching anyone but Erik.

Jared laughed out loud, his face split with an ear-to-ear grin. When he finally got himself under control he wiped the tears from his eyes and sucked in air. "I was going to ask if you were interested in a little advice. Sweetie, if you're scented to the Beta, I'm not going anywhere near you in a sexual way, even if you beg. I'd like to keep the family jewels intact and usable for a few more years."

She didn't think she could be any more embarrassed. All she'd done lately had been jump to conclusions. "Sorry." When she lifted her gaze, he was still grinning. "So, what's your advice?"

Jared shrugged. "You don't seem to know much about him. The mate thing is supposed to be cool, as in being positive they're the only one for you. Yada yada. It works, I've seen it with the Alphas, and with others in the pack. I still think there's nothing wrong with a little good old-fashioned conversation to go along with the instant physical attraction and the lifelong chemical bond."

Maggie stood stunned for a moment.

"What? You look like I just suggested the two of you go bite heads off live chickens or something."

She snorted. "I'll confess your advice is not what I expected."

Jared adjusted the straps on his pack and pointed up the trail. He resumed talking as she walked beside him. "Why? Because you heard I like the ladies? I do, and if you weren't taken I'd be doing my damnedest to romance you. But I'm not stupid, I like more than a tumble. Sex is fun, but my hand is a lot safer than a regular routine of loving and leaving without more than a howdy-do and goodbye."

Maggie walked in silence for a minute before facing him. "That's good advice."

He winked. "But if you're *not* mates, then..."

She swung at him, and he danced ahead of her, laughing.

She took a deep breath and followed. These wolves were different from what she remembered in her teen years. The posturing and constant one-upmanship weren't there. It must be because they were involved in the Games. This couldn't be how they lived all the time.

Could it?

TJ and Erik disappeared from the top of the next rise, heading off the trail into the bush. They must have found another clue. By the time she'd reached the heights, the guys were back, Erik sporting a rather large grin.

"You found another one?" Without thinking, Maggie leaned against him to check out the paper in his hand. His body was warm and solid, and she adjusted herself to nestle closer, tugging until the clue sheet was within her vision.

He chuckled, and she suddenly realized she was completely inside the circle of his arms. When she would have retreated, he subtly closed the space and trapped her, drawing her attention to the paper.

"Number eight. I tell you, the clues are logical, but if TJ didn't have such a good sense of smell I think we would have missed half of them."

TJ lay flat out on the trail, panting lightly. His ears pricked up when Erik said his name, as if delighted by the praise.

Jared dropped his pack and passed out granola bars, unwrapping TJ's and tossing it to him whole. "Where was the clue this time?"

"On a tree."

"Drawn on?"

Erik shook his head. "Carved into the bark. Looks like it was done at least six months ago."

Jared swore. "How the hell did TJ get a scent on something that old? That's freaky impossible."

Maggie stared down at TJ. She could have sworn he winked at her.

Erik laughed. "Yeah. The kid has always said his sniffer was good, and he wasn't kidding. We're at the point I think we should set up camp. I'd like to make an early start tomorrow so we have enough time at the end of the day to figure out the first mental challenge."

"You want to camp here?" Jared looked around. Maggie wondered too—there wasn't much of a clearing.

"Sheep Camp should be within the next half hour of hiking. Let's make that our destination. Once we get there, TJ can shift back, and we'll get supper going." Erik turned to her and Maggie froze. He adjusted her chest harness straps then patted her cheek with his fingers before pointing for her to follow TJ's lead. She stared at him even as her body obeyed, and she took her first steps still watching his face. There was a laughing look in his eyes that made her want to haul him aside and ask just what the hell was going on.

She walked in silence for almost twenty minutes before it hit her. She'd spent the entire day with pack members, one in wolf, and she wasn't having a panic attack. She hadn't passed out and she was still safe.

Maybe Missy had been right. Maybe it was time to move on.

~

"So what do you think this is?"

Jared hit TJ over the head with his baseball cap. "Shut.

Up. That's why it's called a puzzle, you idiot, because we don't know what it means."

"Jared." Erik didn't want to have to deal with a couple of young punks right now. Maggie reclined next to him and her scent filled the air. He'd far prefer to be able to continue the little mental fantasy he'd been enjoying than have to discipline his teammates.

"But he's asked the same damn question ten times already."

Erik sighed, sitting up with reluctance. "I know. I'm only four feet away, and I've heard him every single bloody time. As well as heard you make smart-ass responses and guesses back every single bloody time." He held out his hand. "Give me the puzzle page and find something else to occupy your minds. We don't have enough clues to be able to solve this, and you're both getting on my nerves."

The two young men exchanged panicked glances and then got busy. Jared grabbed a knife and whittled at a stick, while TJ produced a mouth organ from somewhere and started playing some pretty damn good blues. Erik always had appreciated that—even though TJ was clumsy, everywhere he went, music followed.

Erik was just about to settle back down when there was a soft touch on his arm.

"You did that well."

Maggie sat with her arms wrapped around her legs, her face whiter than he remembered. *Shit.* "Did I scare you? I didn't mean to. The boys know I'm joking around."

She shook her head and frowned. "I'm not upset."

"You look pale." He shut his mouth quickly. What an incredibly stupid thing to say.

She rolled her eyes at him. "Gee, thanks. You're really batting a thousand right now aren't you?"

Yup. "Are you tired? Hungry?"

Can I massage your feet—or any other part of your body?
What he wouldn't give to be able to touch her. The whole
day spent together, even hiking, had made his desire for her
rise.

"No, I had more than enough at supper. I just need to
think for a bit. Thanks for asking the comedy duo to shut
up. I haven't been around a lot of people for a while and
their constant yattering was getting to me." She stretched
lazily, and he enjoyed the way her T-shirt pulled tight over
her breasts, the display making his mouth water. She might
be a little thing, especially compared to him, but her breasts
were full and distracting.

She curled up next to him, her hip touching his, and he
smiled. There was no way to ignore the physical pull
between them. He wasn't even interested in trying to act as
if it wasn't there. He'd go as slow as she needed, but he
wouldn't back down.

For the next thirty minutes he pretended to stare at the
puzzle clues all the while looking over every inch of her
body. She was going to be his—to care for and love and be
with for the rest of their lives. The whole idea of fated
mates didn't bother him one bit.

Jared yawned, a loud juicy sound that made Erik laugh.
Time to round them up. "Hey, good job today, everyone."

TJ waved lazily, tucking away the mouth organ and
letting out his own yawn. "It's the altitude, I swear it is. I'm
heading to bed. Early morning I assume?"

"On the trail by seven."

Jared nodded. "I'll turn in as well. I need to spend some
time *talking* to my eyelids."

Erik wondered what the hell was up as Jared directed a
pointed look at Maggie as he spoke, and she laughed.

It took a long time for the boys to crawl into the tent, and organize their sleeping bags with all their goofing off. The grumbles and laughter slowly died away, and Erik relaxed. Finally. Time alone with his mate.

The two of them sat silently, the small noises of the forest at night continuing. Here in the southernmost part of the Yukon, the sky insisted on staying bright, but it wasn't midnight sun by any means. There was a beautiful pink glow rising from behind the western mountains and Erik shuffled back down to rest his head on the log they'd rolled over to sit on.

Maggie looked at him for a long moment before sighing. "It's no use, is it?"

"What?"

She touched his arm hesitantly, and a thrill shot through him. *Oh hell-o.* He kept his hands behind his head and watched as she wiggled closer, resting her head on his chest. Her hair tickled his chin and her breath warmed him. "I can't deny I'm attracted to you. My wolf likes you too." She sat up to look into his eyes. "I just can't..."

"I'm not asking you to. Not yet. You told me to wait, I'm waiting." Shit, crap, and merde, he was waiting.

"Where were you born?"

Erik blinked. "That was a quick change of topic."

She snuggled against him, and his wolf preened at the attention. "I just thought maybe if we learned a little more about each other, it would help."

He nodded slowly. Made sense. Didn't seem like they were going to be passing the time with any other distracting activities.

"Lavrentiya. Small coastal village on the Bering Strait."

She paused. "I guess that explains why you speak Russian. When did you come to Alaska?"

He told her about his childhood and moving around until the family finally settled in Sitka. "The rest of my family is still there. I'd love to take you to meet them. When this is all over."

"All over?"

"The Games."

"Oh." She nodded. "That would be...nice. I guess."

"What about you? I know your family went through some tough times, so let's not talk about that now. Tell me your favorite colour."

Maggie snorted. "You're really not what I expected, you know that?"

"Why? Because I want to be able to buy you sexy underwear in your favorite colour?" Her jaw dropped and he grinned. "Damn, you're fun to tease." She wiggled her nose and he wondered what was going on behind those beautiful eyes of hers.

He grabbed her hand. He'd done more handholding in the past few days than in his entire life before. "I was thinking about your fainting issue while we were on the trail. You said it's a chemical imbalance?"

She nodded. "It only got bad this past year, and obviously I can't shift to wolf for her to be able to heal me."

Yeah, that part. He wasn't even going to try to touch that issue yet. Soon, but not tonight. "I think it has to do with you not shifting and avoiding wolves. We give off so many pheromones, all the time, it helps maintain a delicate balance. Now that you're around pack, even a few of us, you should feel better."

Maggie stared at him. "That's why I came north to rejoin the pack. Missy insisted being around her family would be enough to heal me." She looked down at where their joint hands rested in his lap. "How did you figure it out? Do you have training in chemistry or something?"

"Nope. PhD in Slavic languages." She gasped in surprise, her eyes widening, and he laughed at her expression. "With a master's in Classic Literature."

"But...you work with Keil as a wilderness guide."

He shrugged. "When he looked into starting the company, he knew his brother would be too young to be a real help for a number of years. I offered to partner with him until TJ is able to take over."

"But why, if you have all this education..."

Maggie wrinkled her brow, and he smoothed the skin on her forehead with his thumb. "He's my best friend. I'm currently tutoring a half-dozen students online, so I'm still using my skills, but it would have been very selfish to let his dream die when I could help him."

Her bright eyes examined his face closely, as if she was trying to see if this was some kind of trick to impress her. "You're a very complicated man, Erik Costanov."

He shook his head. "I'm as simple as they come. I believe in the golden rule, and I try to live by it."

She knocked him off balance by crawling across his legs and straddling him, her butt resting on his thighs. He lay very still, afraid to scare her, but savouring the sensation of her weight on top of him.

"What are you doing?" There, that managed to come out sounding reasonably intelligible. Damn, he spoke seven languages and right now English didn't seem to be one of them. His tongue was glued to the roof of his mouth.

She wiggled a little closer and he bit back a groan. Her hot core now rested against his groin and his cock rose like new bread in an oven. "I want to kiss you."

Hallelujahs rang in his brain. Holy freaking

exclamations of jubilation, rejoicing and unending glee broke out in a full chorus. But when he spoke, he delivered a measured, "Okay."

She leaned forward and brushed her lips over his, and the electric sensation he'd felt before when they kissed buzzed through his torso and up his spine to his brain. Before he knew it, he'd buried the fingers of one hand in her hair, moving her the way he wanted her, while the other wrapped around her body to pull their torsos together. Her sweetness filled his senses, tantalizing his taste buds with the desire for more. Eager noises rose from her as their tongues brushed.

The night remained warm, and they both wore only shorts and T-shirts. Having a barrier between them was torture.

He broke off their kiss, sat with her still straddling him, and whipped off his shirt. Her eyes bulged for a second before she reached down to caress his abdomen, the fleeting strokes tormenting him even as he savoured his mate finally, *finally* touching his skin again.

"Please take off your shirt." His voice cracked, he needed this so much. He closed his eyes against the disappointment of her saying no, then the rustle of fabric hit his ears. When he looked again, she still wore her bra, but the creamy smoothness of the rest of her skin more than made up for that small disappointment. He touched her reverently, stroking from her hips up the gentle indent of her waist until he covered the swells of her lace-covered breasts.

She sucked in a gasp as he rubbed his thumbs in small circles over her nipples, the tips beading to tight points that stabbed his flesh through the fabric. "You're beautiful."

He ignored the driving urge to roll her over and take

her, and instead slipped his hands back around her torso so their lips met again.

They kissed leisurely, exploring each other's mouths and necks, tongues stroking, teeth nibbling. Erik wasn't sure how long they sat there and frankly, he didn't give a damn. He'd waited his whole life for her, and they were finally doing what his wolf had been howling at him to do for days. Although the beast was going to be sorely disappointed when they didn't go all the way.

Maggie's breathing grew more rapid and she squirmed against him, her mound rubbing his groin like a firebrand. When he finally couldn't take it anymore, he grabbed her by the ass and adjusted her until he was happy. He ground them together again and again, and she moaned in his ear. Damn, he was going to come right like this if he didn't watch it.

So he lifted her and undid her belt.

She slapped at his hands. "What are you doing?"

"Take off your pants."

"Erik, we can't—"

He was on fire with a desperate need. "We're not having sex but I need to touch you. Take them off, now," he demanded. Begged.

She hesitated for just a second, then unzipped and dropped both her panties and her shorts, stepping out of the legs where they bunched around her ankles. She stood there, bare-naked except for her bra, with her pussy right in front of him, and he had no power to resist.

He clutched her ass and buried his face between her legs. She cried out softly, but he was too busy to warn her to stay quiet. Her sweet scent drew him, and he separated the curls covering her with his tongue and licked the length of her slit.

Oh Lord, she tasted good. Her flavour raced through him and drugged his senses. He pressed his tongue into her pussy as far as it would go, lapping at the cream coating her passage.

She rocked against his mouth, opening her legs wider, her fingers clutching his head. The arm he'd wrapped around her ensured she stayed right where he could reach and delve into her body. She made the most delicious noises, and he stopped to take a deep breath and enjoy the sensation of holding her intimately.

"More," she demanded.

"Yes." He slipped a finger into her depths and suckled her clit with his mouth.

"*Yessss...*" Her hiss of agreement trailed off into the contented rumble of a wolf being petted and he smiled.

He knew how to wake her wolf. When Maggie was ready, they would call her up together. For now, he wanted to bring his mate pleasure and concentrated all his attention on her. He teased the lips of her pussy with his fingers, circling the tender folds, before again plunging one, then two fingers in and out of her sheath. Running his tongue around the swollen bud of her clit, he flicked it repetitively with the hardened tip of his tongue.

A trembling started in her thighs, her knees shook and he lapped harder. He supported her with one hand as she cried out with her orgasm, a howling keen of delight that echoed into the still-bright sky.

He dragged his fingers from her body with reluctance, the sticky moisture covering his hand calling like an aphrodisiac. He held her hips, giving her time to recover. The hands clasping his head softened their death grip as she caressed his short hair. He closed his eyes and planted a kiss on the tender skin in the crease of her thigh. Her scent filled every cell of his body and stopping now was the hardest thing he'd ever done.

A gentle tap on his cheek brought his attention to her bright eyes filled with passion and gratitude. "That was amazing."

"For us both."

She giggled. "I guess this proves I really am a wolf at heart. Damn, I can't even feel embarrassed everyone within a five-mile radius knows I just climaxed."

They laughed together as Erik pulled up her undies and helped her with her shorts. Their hands brushed and bumped and tangled as he took advantage of every touch he could sneak in.

She dropped back onto his lap, her arms draped around his neck. "Thank you."

"My pleasure." It had been. Her gaze dropped to his crotch and the obvious swell remaining behind the fabric. "Yes, I still want you."

Maggie nibbled on her lower lip. "Not yet. I'm sorry, it's so selfish, but I'm not ready."

"But soon?"

She hesitated. "Maybe."

His heart leapt. *Maybe* was way up from *no*. "I can live with maybe."

He kissed her one last time, just to drive himself insane, then led her to the tent. Morning would come soon enough.

7

—————

"We've got a problem."

Maggie groaned as she sat up from where she'd sprawled on the side of the trail. The past two hours had been sheer hell as they slogged their way to the top of the Golden Stairs and over the Chilkoot Pass. She hadn't hiked so much vertical ascent since she was a teenager, and every muscle screamed in protest. "What's wrong, Jared?"

"Did TJ lose a page of the puzzle when he was goofing off last night?" Jared frowned as he flipped through pages. Erik reached out and Jared handed them over. Maggie watched in concern as Erik examined the set. Jared growled in frustration. "If King Klutz—"

"That's enough." Erik cut in sternly, and Jared had the grace to look sheepish. "There's nothing missing. What's the issue?"

"There are no additional clues for the last few spaces," Jared pointed out. "There are also no landmark clues. Three completely blank columns—it's like we're going in blind and have to find a needle in a haystack."

Maggie crawled closer to look over Erik's shoulder at the papers. She leaned against his strong back, the warmth of his body drawing her like a magnet. The whole day she'd forced herself to stay away from him, but now gave in to the need to recharge her batteries with a brief touch. He glanced at her and winked, and she blushed. Their sexual attraction was normal for wolves, but her continued denial of their mating and his patient response confused her. She felt like a broken fan, running hot then cold.

"I noticed the first day. We'll figure it out tonight." Erik handed the papers back to Jared. The young man stared in shock.

"How can we fill in the missing answers without clues or landmarks? Why didn't you say something earlier?"

Erik shrugged. "There was no use in panicking. The challenge must be solvable, so I decided we'd figure it out as we went along."

Jared shook his head. "You really are too cool and collected at times, aren't you?"

A muffled howl rose from up the trail, and they turned to see TJ racing back. His loping gait tore up the rocky terrain as he returned to drop a rock at their feet.

Erik picked it up, running a hand over TJ's head. "Well done. I wasn't looking forward to hunting for this answer."

"Where was it?"

He pointed to the mountain spine extending another mile off to their left, the razor edge jagged against the skyline. "The puzzle clue was *Cutting you off*, and the map shows the location to be along the far ridge. I sent TJ ahead in the hopes the answer would be something obvious and save the rest of us the trip."

Maggie swallowed hard. Imagining having to hike the

ragged rocks to the spire made her even more grateful for TJ's wolf. "I would never have made that."

"What symbol do I add?" Jared asked.

Erik handed the rock over to Maggie and she turned it over carefully. "There's nothing carved on it." Her stomach fell. Were they going to have to do the dangerous climb after all?

"Don't worry, this is what we need. It's not always simple like having the answer written on the surface. Remember the answer to the sixth clue involved a math formula." Erik nudged her arm. "What kind of rock is it?"

TJ pawed at her feet, and she knelt to scratch behind his ears as she stared at the stone chip. "You wouldn't have brought it unless you thought it was the answer, so I'll assume it wasn't in a normal setting." She wrinkled her nose. "It sparkles, so I'll guess it's fool's gold. There's got to be a lot in these parts."

Erik laughed. "Remind me never to go panning with you. You'd miss out on a bonanza."

She gaped at him. "It's *real* gold?"

"Yup, and that's not the usual location to find a nugget. Gold is rarely found loose like this, and never up that high. Someone had to have planted it there."

Maggie rotated the chunk again. "Still doesn't look like much to me."

Jared added a few notes with a flourish. "One piece of gold." He glanced up, worry back on his face. "There's only three more clues before we run out and hit the blank section of the puzzle."

"Then we'll stop for the night." Erik rose and held out a hand to Maggie to assist her up. She took it gratefully. "That's the last of the big uphill. From here on it's rolling trail until we start down to Bennett Lake. The next clue is

Reflections and the coordinates look like it should be by a water source, so let's get moving. The day will be done before we know it."

He held up her backpack. Maggie crawled under the shoulder straps reluctantly. He brushed his hands over her body as he helped tighten the snaps and buckles, and her skin tingled.

"Stop it," she whispered. Great, now she was going to be hiking with sore feet, tired muscles and an aching need in her belly.

Erik chuckled. "I'm just trying to be helpful."

She elbowed him.

∼

"BUT IT DOESN'T MEAN ANYTHING." TJ scratched his head.

"It has to." Jared paced back and forth and Maggie rubbed her temples. They'd set up camp two hours ago, had dinner and then the puzzle began to drive them all nuts.

"They are totally unrelated words. It's gibberish, no matter which way we read them."

Maggie stared at the papers at her feet. It was true. There was no logic in any of the words and symbols they'd found. "We've tried rearranging the words. We've taken the first letter, the last letter. We've..."

"...tried *everything*." Jared glanced at Erik. "What if we don't figure this out? Can we finish without the last six clues?"

Erik nodded slowly. "We just need to get to the Bennett Lake check-in by three o'clock. That's not a problem at all. Only in previous Games, the final challenge used information gathered from all the rest of the events. Five years ago the team in fourth spot came from behind to win because none of the leaders had all the clues."

Maggie sighed. She'd felt so useless this whole challenge. Unlike TJ who had more than pulled his weight, all she'd done was ensure they hiked slower than usual.

Usually she was good at logic puzzles. She picked up the clues and shuffled through them again. Something caught her eye.

"Erik, what are these notes?"

He sat next to her, and she soaked in his presence. "Those? I kept track of where we found the answer. I figured everything might help in the end."

Her heart raced. "What if the clues weren't just to help us find the location, but we have to use them twice?"

Jared plopped down across from them, hope shining on his face. "How do you use a clue twice?"

Maggie laid out the paper and pointed. "We found the answer to number eleven by looking in the reflection of the pool at the base of the waterfall, right?"

"There was the Greek symbol omega. We wrote it down. It means nothing."

She nodded. "But when you look at your reflection it comes out backwards." She wanted to jump up and down. This was the right track, she was sure of it.

Erik brushed her arm. "But the symbol for omega is the same whether you draw it backward or forward."

Maggie laughed. "But what if you think of it as the back of the alphabet? Omega is the last letter of the Greek alphabet. What's at the other end?"

TJ shot up his arm before lowering it slowly. "Sorry, too many years of school training. Alpha is the Greek A."

"Right." Maggie started a new paper. She deliberately drew the symbol for alpha. "And here...we wrote down *gold.*

But the clue said *Cutting you off*. The chemical formula for gold is Au. If we cut off the U we get an A."

The next thirty minutes passed in a blur as they struggled through the rest of the puzzle, discovering as they fed the current answer through the clue again there were clear-cut alternatives.

"In your notes you recorded what height we found the answers, high up or low to the ground. Should I add that information?" Maggie glanced at Erik to find him staring at her with a twinkle in his eyes. "What?"

"You're very attractive when you're obsessed about something."

Jared laughed. "You two. Save the lovey-dovey for later. Let's solve this thing."

When the new list was finished, Maggie held it up with a flourish. Now they would be able to find the final answers. She scanned the page quickly and her hopes fell. There was nothing but a series of single letters from A-G mixed up again and again.

It still made no sense.

Jared and TJ started laughing, and her temper flared.

"It's not funny." So much for her being an asset to the team like Erik had suggested.

"We tried. I guess we'll just have to finish without the final information." Jared threw a rock into the bush and lay back on the ground in disgust.

TJ startled. "What are you guys talking about? Don't you see it?"

His earnest expression made Maggie feel even worse. "There's nothing there that helps us, TJ."

He snorted before stealing the paper from her to scrawl down six more letters.

Erik looked at the list and raised a brow. "You think?"

"Positive." TJ nodded rapidly. He scrambled in his pockets, fumbling as he pulled out his harmonica.

As the first notes of the familiar children's opera rang into the air on the unusual wind instrument, Maggie laughed. "No way, you're saying those letters are musical notes? That tune is too funny."

Erik grinned at her. "I think TJ's hit on the right solution. Does it help if I tell you the race director's name is Peter?" He clapped slowly. "Well done, team."

Jared groaned. "'Peter and the Wolf'? We went through all that searching to have to listen to TJ playing bad classical music on his harmonica?"

TJ hit him, and the two of them tumbled away to wrestle again. Erik smiled down at her and she grinned back in satisfaction. She really had managed to help the team.

Suddenly the idea of being a part of the pack didn't nauseate her. The guys had been nothing but supportive of her, and her heart no longer went into palpitations when she remembered she was in the bush with three other wolves.

Except for the rushing, pounding rapid beat of her heart that remained every time she thought about Erik.

Her wolf bumped to the surface, as if reaching for him. His eyes widened as they stared at each other, and Maggie had to hold back from pressing closer, rubbing herself all over him. For one moment she seriously considered dragging him into the tent and accepting their mating.

Her throat closed tight and she dropped her gaze away, fidgeting with the papers. She organized them, then thrust them at him.

The idea of being in wolf form with others around—she wasn't sure she'd ever be ready for that step. Mating with Erik but refusing to let their wolves have contact would be the cruelest thing imaginable. She couldn't play games with his emotions, couldn't tease his wolf with promises she was unable to keep.

What of the challenges still to come in the Wolf Games? Had she helped solve this puzzle only to tear victory from their grasp when she was unable to shift?

"You're thinking too hard. Let it rest." Erik brushed a stray hair back behind her ear, and she leaned into the caress without thinking. "In fact we all should turn in. Just because we know what we're looking for won't make tomorrow any easier."

"So using the song to solve the puzzle gave us six letters in the answer column, but no idea where we'll find them? I assume that's the information we'll need for the final event, right? That sucks," Jared complained as he unzipped the fly to the tent.

"Hey, at least we know what to look for, and with TJ's great sense of smell, I'm confident we'll be at the checkpoint in plenty of time." Erik patted TJ on the back, catching him by the shirt when he tripped. "Yup, a good night's sleep and a short hike tomorrow. I'm betting there will be little time between the end of this challenge and the start of the next."

Erik settled the boys, returning to hold his hand out to her. "As much as I'd love a repeat of last night, I suggest we hit the sack as well."

She nodded slowly. There was too much to say and she didn't have the strength yet. "Erik, what if I can't—?"

He held up a hand. "I'm not trying to be rude, but I'd like you to trust me on this one. Sleep first, discussions later. You did so well with the puzzle, but I can feel your exhaustion from here. While you're getting the chemicals you need from being with us, I doubt you've hiked this far in the past few years while hanging out in Vancouver." He pulled her against his body and she molded herself to him. It felt so wonderful. He lifted her chin and stared at her. "I'm warning you I'm going to hold you tonight. I can't resist, and I think you need it too. If you were planning on protesting, argue here so we don't wake the boys."

Jared's snores already rocked the tent and Maggie laughed. "Like me blowing a trumpet in his ear would wake him." They exchanged grins before she grew serious again. There was nothing she wanted more right now than to feel his arms around her. "I could handle you holding me. If you feel you absolutely must."

He nodded seriously. "I think it's vital."

They slipped into the tent and Maggie relaxed, the warmth of her mate covering her like a blanket as the never-ending light shone through the walls of the tent, filling the space with a peaceful blue glow.

8

---

*E*rik was pleased when their team finished the challenge in plenty of time, finding all but one of the puzzle pieces. Maggie had insisted on recording everything she could think of about the locations where they'd discovered the letters, hoping the information would help them down the road.

They'd barely crossed the line at the checkpoint before being whisked away to Carmacks to start the next race.

He kept Maggie beside him as they boarded the bus with four other teams. The fear in her eyes made his heart ache, but the way she squared her shoulders and insisted on sitting with TJ filled him with pride.

The chairman rose at the front of the bus to announce the details of the next challenge.

"You'll all be in human form for this event of the Games."

A murmur carried through the bus, and TJ swore under his breath. Erik dropped a reassuring hand on the young man's shoulder.

"You'll be paddling through one of the toughest sections

of the Yukon River. Because of changing water levels, the Five Finger Rapids are nowhere near as dangerous as they were in the days of the Gold Rush. But we've planned a mass start, so there will be a lot of canoes vying for the safest route. It's up to you to make it through to the other side in one piece.

"Scoring for this event will involve both time and bonus points. There will also be deductions." He held up a brightly coloured float. "We've got six buoys anchored at various points along the river. If you get close enough, you'll once again have an opportunity to observe a symbol that will help you later. It's completely discretionary if you wish to attempt to reach the buoys."

"What would cause a deduction?" one of the Anchorage team asked.

The chairman grinned, his canines long and sharp. "Falling out of the canoe. You can still get a time score when your canoe crosses the finish line, but anyone out of the canoe causes a deduction to be applied, no matter how it happens."

TJ's shoulder tensed even more under Erik's hand. The kid was just going to have to get over his fear of screwing up. So he was clumsy—he was way better now than a few years ago.

The chairman sat, and a low rumble of voices filled the bus. Erik leaned back in his seat trying to get comfortable for the journey, his knees cramped against the back of the bench in front of him. Even the buses adapted for wolves were too small for his bulk. He sighed and closed his eyes.

When he opened them again they'd arrived at Carmacks.

He herded his crew over to the side of the staging area, then stood back to take a good look at the setup. The canoes were lined up along the edge of the river, twenty feet from the shoreline. Erik eyed his opponents with a practiced eye, spotting the three teams who would be the most competition in this event.

TJ remained silent as Jared joked around. Without her saying a word, Erik knew exactly where Maggie stood, hiding behind his back, sneaking peeks around him at the other wolves. She was doing extraordinarily well, not panicking as the group grew larger by the minute. All the teams were assembled, and their support crews were placing the final supplies in piles for the teams to collect, when the whistle sounded.

Arms wrapped around his waist and he stilled, covering her small hands with his own. She'd buried her face in his back, her breath warm against his skin. Small tremors shook her body, and he twisted, kneeling to enclose her in his embrace. They stayed there for a moment, just breathing each other's air. It felt so damn right to hold her.

He kissed her forehead gently. "You okay?"

She nodded quickly. "I might throw up a few times, but I'm not giving up." Her stubborn announcement made his heart sing. They were truly going to be a wonderful pair, once they dealt with a few minor issues like her shifting problem. Her refusal to accept their mating. Making sure—

Jared nudged them, breaking them apart, before handing over two life jackets. "Try to throw up over the edge of the gunwales."

Maggie smacked Jared on the arm. "Next time, don't listen to a private conversation. If I have to throw up, I'll throw up anywhere I damn well please. Got it?"

A ripple of shock crossed Jared's face, and he dipped his head in submission. Maggie stood just a little straighter, and

Erik hid his grin. It seemed his little wolf was starting to feel her place in the pack.

He turned to make sure TJ had his lifejacket on properly. The boy was still swearing colourfully, with few repetitions.

"Does your brother know you're this talented with words?"

TJ snorted. "Who do you think I learned them from? Well, him and Robyn. She's awful good at cussing in sign language."

"What's wrong?"

"I'm going to fuck this up. I just know it. I'm going to cause some major catastrophe."

"Why?"

TJ looked at him like he'd grown a third head. "Because I'm *me*. You know I can't walk twenty feet without landing on my face."

Erik shrugged. "You bounce pretty good. Just get up and get your ass into the boat." He tightened TJ's lifejacket straps then stepped back to complete his own.

TJ continued to stare. "How can you be so calm when chances are I'm about to screw this up for us like I always—"

"Enough." Erik let his power envelop the young man he towered over. "I don't let anyone talk shit about you, not even you. Do your best. That's all any of us ask. If you do have an accident then fix it the best way you can."

The panic in TJ's eyes faded slightly.

A piercing whistle broke the air, and the team gathered around Erik.

"Okay, there's the five-minute warning. Those are prospector canoes—flat bottomed, so they're nice and stable. I want Jared in front, TJ and Maggie side by side in the middle. I'll take the stern and steer us. What do you think about going for the extra buoys? Yes or no?"

TJ flicked a glance at the team. "I'm just going to paddle and keep my ass in the seat. I'll do whatever you decide."

Maggie chewed on her lip. "Are the buoys far out of our path?"

Erik shook his head. "Looks like we can pretty much stick to the current. We'll want to do that anyway to make the best time. The fastest route down the river is not a straight line. When we get close to the rocks, we'll have to stay to the right." He looked at Maggie. "Did you ever see the rapids when you lived in Whitehorse?"

"If I did, it was a long time ago."

"There are four towers of granite that divide the river into five parts. The far right is the best one to go through, but the main thing is to avoid the towers themselves, and the far-left channels. There are sweepers off the left, and some nasty undercurrents over there. When we get close, just listen to my instructions. We'll use the first few minutes in the canoe to practice our strokes."

"What about the symbols?" Jared jiggled on the spot as he stood waiting.

"Maggie, I want you to try to memorize them. Describe them out loud when you see them and we'll all try to help remember, but I don't want all four of us staring at the damn things or we'll be in the drink for sure."

The final warning whistle blew and there was no more time for discussion. The gun went off and they were away, racing over the grass to grab paddles. They sprinted to the side of the canoe, manhandling it down to the water's edge. Jared hopped in, TJ fell in and Maggie gracefully jumped over the side as he pushed them out into the current.

"I hate wet socks." Jared complained from the front of the canoe.

Maggie peeked at his feet. "You're not wearing socks."

Erik laughed. "Okay. Practice time. Everyone draw on the right."

They practiced maneuvering the canoe until Erik felt they should at least survive the trip. The rest of the competitors had settled into a pattern around them. There were two canoes alone in the lead, a group of six or seven close around the Granite Lake team, and another larger pack behind them.

"Buoy approaching on the right," Jared shouted.

Erik checked the river. "We'll try for this one, then we need to slip to the left more."

Three other canoes all veered the same direction, and suddenly the river grew crowded. Erik angled their craft, but it was too late. One canoe rammed them in the bow, another slammed the opposite side.

"Shit." TJ's paddle went flying. He managed to grab the seat, the boat rocking as he fought to regain his balance.

Erik ruddered hard, even as Maggie's quiet voice rose over the shouts of the other teams. "I saw the symbol. We can go."

They pulled away from the mess of boats.

Once they were back in the current, Erik reached under his feet and poked the swearing TJ in the back with a spare paddle.

"You eat with that mouth? Here." The look of delight on TJ's face made Erik grin. "Just hold on to it tight, okay? We've only got one spare left."

"I thought you were going to call out the symbols, Maggie?" Jared glanced over his shoulder at her.

"I figured just in case someone didn't see it, I shouldn't

announce it for them all. It looked like a cowboy hat with a triangle underneath."

The crowd of boats slowly spread out. Clusters of twos and threes still paddled beside each other, but with each buoy Granite Lake managed to lose another of their closest competitors. They made it past three more buoys before Erik decided it was enough.

"The rapids are around this corner. Let's concentrate on finishing strong and not worry about the final clues."

The team was silent for a moment before Maggie spoke. "I *am* getting tired."

Jared nodded. "I vote for finishing. If you noticed the canoes ahead of us, not one of them stopped to get any of the extra clues. I think the four we saw is enough."

They settled into a paddling pattern. There was a certain joy in moving in synchronization with the group this way. Not as good as running in a pack, but with a rhythm and a beauty to it all the same. Erik admired Maggie's arms and shoulders as she paddled, watching the way her muscles moved under the skin.

He'd love to see her body shifting like that on top of him, rocking from side to—*damn*. This was not the time to get distracted thinking about his mate.

He steered them toward the safest channel just as a loud ruckus behind them made him check over his shoulder.

Shit.

"Holy crap! Did you see that?" Jared gasped.

"Eyes forward, Jared. You need to keep to your task as lookout."

"But they dumped the other team!"

Erik shook his head. "Keep paddling, crew. Yeah, we've got a group trying an unusual method to gain points. Concentrate on the river in front of us, and let me worry about the cheaters." TJ and Maggie exchanged worried glances before paddling madly. "Whoa, no rush. Just paddle. Trust me."

Erik laughed silently. He'd wondered when someone would get creative. While wolves followed a strict code of conduct in governance, one of the sub-rules was if you were powerful enough, you could make your own rules.

Another shout rose from behind, and he watched for a moment as the cheating team came alongside their next victim and made short work of tipping them over.

Erik considered a defense and decided they'd never know what hit them. "TJ, remember when we guided that family reunion down the Stikine?"

"Are you freaking kidding? I still have nightmares...oh no. Holy shit, you can't be serious—?"

"On my command."

"Crapola. Yes, sir."

"Erik. What's happening?" Maggie sounded frightened and he wanted to reassure her, but there was no time. In a rush the other canoe was at their side, three of their team all at the ready to grasp the side of the Granite Lake craft.

"Now?" TJ asked, his voice coming out high and squeaky.

"Wait for it." Erik glanced at the captain in the rear. He should have known. "Darren. Having a good time so far? You and the team?" There weren't many people Erik actively disliked, but Darren topped his shit list.

The captain of the Anchorage team startled at Erik's bland comment, then grinned widely, his canines showing. "Wonderful time. We'll see you at the finish line, dripping wet."

Erik shrugged. "If you insist. Now, TJ."

TJ leapt, his long limbs propelling him into the air and over the side. He came down hard in the neighbouring boat.

Maggie squealed as their canoe rocked. Jared dropped into the bottom to help stabilize it. Erik threw himself down as well, cracking his paddle on the knuckles of the other team where they clasped the gunwales.

Shouts of pain rang out, the hands released and with a clatter the boats sprang apart.

"What the hell—?" Darren's angry shout was followed by an enormous splash.

Erik, Maggie and Jared sat up slowly to watch the opposing team flounder around their capsized craft. Somehow their canoe had flipped over completely. TJ clung precariously to the bottom, his arms and knees spread like he was in wolf form. Erik snickered in appreciation at Darren's expression until a change in the roar of water alerted him.

They all spun to see the towers of rock rapidly approaching. They grabbed their paddles and slid back into position.

"Draw on the right, Maggie. Jared, forward on the left. Don't panic, we've got time."

"What about TJ?" Maggie asked, concern in her voice.

"He's probably going to get wet. We figured it was a very real possibility from the start. Hard! Paddle hard!" Erik judged the distance to the approaching rocks. Finally they were in the correct line. *Good.* They still had time. "Back paddle. Now."

The rush of water forced them forward no matter how much they struggled against it, but there was enough difference in momentum that the canoe carrying TJ caught up to them. It could all be for nothing if this didn't work.

Erik knelt on the bottom, his knees spread wide to try to reduce the rocking. "When I call out, brace yourselves."

He took a deep breath, reached out a hand and grabbed TJ's wrist. "Now!"

One solid yank brought TJ flying across the space between the canoes, his arms and legs flailing wildly. He landed in a heap in front of Erik, gasping for air as the other canoe flipped and filled with water.

"Erik!" Jared shouted a warning.

There was no time to do anything but pick up his paddle and slam it into the water. Erik leaned hard, using the blade like a rudder, steering them away from the rapidly approaching rock formation.

Jared whooped as a sudden cross-eddy dragged them past the jagged rock edges to the safety of the downstream side.

They all sat back and let the current carry them, the canoe spiraling in a gradual 360-degree circle. Erik sucked in a calming breath and stared up at the sky. The adrenaline rush faded, his pounding heartbeat slowed.

A loud cheer rose from the people watching along the observation platforms as Granite Lake crossed the finish line. Erik brought them into the docking area set up farther down the river, more than satisfied with his team's efforts.

Maggie and Jared scrambled out first, chatting excitedly as they waited on the dock for him to join them. He picked Maggie up and spun her in a circle, his heart jumping as she gave him a big juicy kiss then hung onto his neck, grinning with delight.

"That was awesome. Can we do it again?"

He laughed. "I knew you had an adventurous streak. You didn't even throw up."

She dropped her head on his shoulder and spoke

quietly. "I'm not happy about being with the other wolves, but being with you feels better and better. I...like you, Erik. I like your sense of justice."

Her confession thrilled him more than finishing another challenge. He squeezed her before carefully putting her down, keeping one arm draped around her shoulders to block her from the other teams walking by.

Glancing into the bottom of the canoe, he found TJ still lying there with his eyes closed, a huge grin pasted on his face.

Erik squatted by the side of the dock. "You planning on coming with us? Because I can send out for a pizza or something if you're staying the night."

TJ opened his eyes and let out a big contented breath. "I didn't screw up, did I?"

Erik laughed. "No. You did just fine."

TJ sat up and nodded. "Maybe there's hope for me after all."

"Maybe." Erik stood and reached for Maggie.

She slapped a hand over her mouth and her eyes popped open wide just as a loud splash rang out. The canoe drifted away down the river as TJ clung to the mooring rope.

He bobbed up and down in the water, swearing softly. A huge sigh escaped him. "Then again, maybe not."

Darren and his team sloshed past, their faces grim. The leader turned to glare at Erik, his gaze raking Maggie's body. Erik stepped in front of her. He didn't want the ass anywhere near her. Not when she'd come so far in facing her fears.

"Nice teamwork, Erik." Darren growled. "You going to introduce me to your lady?"

Maggie ducked under his arm, her face buried against

Erik's side. "Looks like she's not interested. Keep walking, there's nothing here for you."

Darren raised a brow, his gaze flicking between Erik and the little bit of Maggie still showing. "Interesting. We'll see you in the next challenge."

They stomped off, their dripping bodies leaving a trail behind.

$$9$$

Maggie knocked on the door of the hotel room next to hers, her heart beating loud enough she was surprised they couldn't already hear her standing outside. She didn't really want to do this, but since she saw no alternative, she was going to put on her big-girl panties and force herself to have a good time. If she didn't pass out first from nerves.

Jared opened the door and whistled in appreciation. "My oh my, you clean up nice."

Maggie spun in a circle, the layers of her skirt floating around her. Now that she knew he was safe, Jared reminded her of nothing more dangerous than a golden retriever. "Why thank you, kind sir. Is the rest of my harem ready to escort me to the ball?"

He snorted and gestured her in. "TJ's still in the shower, and Erik disappeared thirty minutes ago, saying he needed to grab some stuff."

Maggie sat in the overstuffed chair in the corner of the enormous suite. There was a wet bar behind her, a comfortable sofa facing a massive wall-mounted TV, and an office studio off to the side. "I can't believe they put us in a five-star hotel in Dawson City. I've never experienced the kind of luxury we've had for the past three days."

Jared raised a brow. "What? Just because we're wolves doesn't mean we don't know how to behave in high society." He straightened the collar of his white shirt and pulled on a suit jacket. Maggie admired the results. The boy was a walking advertisement for GQ, wolf style. "Damn, can you help me with this? I can never get it straight."

She slapped his hands out of the way to work on his tie. "Staying here is just such a contrast. They start us with a hike through the wilderness, throw us in the Yukon River and then plant us in Dawson to cool our heels? I mean I've loved the sightseeing and the sleeping in a real bed. And the food...oh my Lord, I've gained ten pounds." She shrugged. "I thought they would make us head right away for the next challenge."

He stepped back to check himself in the mirror. "Remember the Games are supposed to be like the wolf equivalent of the Olympics. Yeah, we all want to do our best, but there's also the good-will-between-packs part. It's a chance to show we can be together without starting territory wars like in the old days."

Maggie collapsed back into the chair. "Jared...I'm going to confess. You guys from the Granite pack are not like any wolves I've met before."

TJ leapt out of the bathroom, stark naked, dripping wet, and singing into a hairbrush at the top of his lungs.

Jared eyed him for a moment before turning to face Maggie, one brow lifted high. "You were saying?"

She burst out laughing. Jared joined her and the two of them gasped for air as TJ stood in the middle of the room, a confused expression on his face. "What?"

The main door opened and Erik wandered in, checking out TJ as he paced around him. "Interesting attire. I take it you're going for the super formal look."

"Ha, ha." TJ dragged a towel over his body then nodded at Erik in his jeans and T-shirt. "What's with you? That's not your usual black-tie outfit."

"Nope."

Maggie rose to examine Erik more closely. The past couple of days he'd been by her side all day long, taking her on tours, buying her trinkets at the souvenir shops. Guarding her when too many wolves crowded around. Then he would kiss her good night outside her hotel room and leave her. Leave her aching and wanting, and she was so ready to rip the clothes right off his gladiator-sized body here and now to sate the urges pulsing through her.

This mate thing was getting seriously out of control.

He winked. "I thought Maggie and I would skip the formal dinner. You two go as the representatives from Granite Lake."

Relief flooded her, the tension headache at the back of her neck slipping away in one smooth stroke. "You mean it?"

He gestured to the basket he'd dropped on the coffee table. "I raided the kitchen. Private picnic for two sound good?"

She threw herself into his arms and buried her face in his neck. She breathed in deeply, his scent filling her head and calming her nerves.

"Thank you," she whispered. He'd known. He'd understood she still couldn't do the whole room full of strange wolves.

Someone cleared their throat, and she realized she was not only clinging to Erik, she'd wrapped her legs around his waist and they were rather intimately pressed together. Not that she was embarrassed—wolves were pretty upfront about sex—but if she didn't move soon, they'd be putting on a show, and she really wanted to be alone with him.

Erik lowered her carefully, brushing his knuckles against her cheek before taking her by the hand. "Boys, I expect you to be on your best behaviour. I don't want to be called back to Diamond Tooth Gertie's and find out you've been fighting."

Jared winked. "Tonight, I'm a lover, not a fighter." He turned to TJ. "Did you see the chick on the Norwegian Team? *Arwhoo.* I claim dibs on that one."

Maggie held tightly to Erik as he whisked her out of the room and down the ornately decorated hallway. "Are we going to get in trouble for not attending?"

He shook his head. "It's an optional event. The guys will have a good time, there will be a lot of sex happening in the corners of the room, and one team will get thrown out for trying to start a rumble. The usual when you get a big gathering of wolves together."

Oh Lord, now she was even happier she didn't have to attend.

They walked quietly down the historic wooden boardwalk, Maggie pulling in long slow breaths of the fresh air. Above them the sky remained daylight bright.

Erik noticed her gazing upward. "We've traveled far enough north sunset won't happen until just after midnight."

She nodded. "I've missed this part of the North. Before we moved away from Whitehorse I used to love staying up late and going for runs…"

Her throat choked tight, and he squeezed her fingers.

He led her into the trees and up a narrow path. By the time they broke out above the city, she could breathe again.

She stood looking down at the narrow streets nestled against the Yukon River, the hills on the other side still showing their scars from the years of dredge mining. The massive machines had followed the hand miners, scooping up layers of rock and soil to shift out every bit of gold, leaving chunks of broken rubble in their wake.

That was her.

Scarred. Beaten, and pulled apart until there was nothing left of value. At least, that's what she'd felt like before meeting Erik. She sighed. If only it was as easy as bulldozing the rocks aside and planting flowers to cover the scars on her heart.

Erik wrapped his arms around her from the back, pulling her against his warm body. "We need to deal with this tonight. I'm pretty sure the next challenge is going to involve us having to shift. We need to talk."

Anger flared. "This is about me being able to shift? For the Games?"

She would have torn herself from his grasp, but suddenly iron bands held her in place.

"Don't. I know you're scared, but don't deliberately try to turn this into a fight to avoid talking to me. I've given you time and space. I just want what's best for you and I don't give a shit if you ever change into a wolf."

He spun her around and clasped her chin, his dark eyes searching hers intently.

"I refuse to stand by and let you face tomorrow unprepared. If I'm right, there will be dozens of wolves surrounding you. I won't allow you to walk into that kind of a situation without me trying to take away a little of your fears. You've asked me to wait before joining with you, and even though it's been hell, I've waited. But don't ask me to not be your mate, to not protect you when I can. Because I won't do it. My wolf won't let me, and neither will my human morals."

She stared at him, her limbs trembling as she realized for the first time she was with someone stronger than her who she could really trust. The ache in her soul urged her on.

"You won't tell Missy?"

He jerked back in surprise. "Doesn't she know?"

She shook her head. "She knows parts, but..." Shame covered her. Her own sister had suffered because of Maggie's weakness.

He spread out the blanket he'd brought, sat and pulled her into his lap. Resting her head against his chest, not looking into his eyes, made it easier to speak. She thought for a moment, then simply told her story.

"I don't know why we moved away from Whitehorse. Mom and Dad died before I got a real answer out of them, but Missy and I always suspected it had something to do with our new Alpha in Whistler. He found out something he held over Dad's head to make him move. Once we were in the pack at Whistler, there was no escape for any of us."

She swallowed hard. "The summer I was seventeen, Missy turned twenty-one. Our Alpha wanted her to marry his brother. He was trying to gain control of her Omega skills, but we didn't know it at the time. Missy only knew Jeff wasn't her mate, and she refused. So they..." She shivered and burrowed deeper into his arms as if his presence could protect her from the memories.

"They came after you?"

She nodded. "I ran. I hid as a human and when they found me, I shifted and ran again. There were six or seven of them, and every time I shifted there was someone in that form to torment me. They hit me." Her voice broke. "They hurt me."

His body tightened under her, indignation and anger pouring off him and forming a protective wall around them. Nothing could touch her right now. He stroked her hair silently for a moment, his heart pounding under her ear.

"Did they rape you?" He spoke softly, gently.

"I don't know!" She squirmed her way back to stare at him. "It sounds so stupid, but I really don't remember. I can feel them grabbing me—my human body—and throwing me on the floor. I shifted, and then there were wolves on top of me, trying to mount me. I shifted back and they tore my skin." She lifted her blouse and twisted to show him the scars along her lower back and her hips. "I shifted so many times in a short period of time I passed out, exhausted from the effort. The next thing I remember is being at home in bed, and Missy telling me she was engaged to Jeff. Dad had made promises to the Alpha, and she was furious. I never said a word, but I know it was my fault she ended up in that marriage. Dad sold her off to save me."

She thought she'd already wept all the tears possible over this. Thought the well had run dry and she had nothing left but a cold stone for a heart. But in Erik's arms, his scent surrounding her, she found sorrows she'd never realized she still clung to. Great racking sobs shook her until she was gasping for air.

Erik rocked her, cradled her, his presence embracing her even closer than his arms. He poured love over her, acceptance. His anger simmering underneath didn't frighten her. It reassured her she would never, ever have to face a situation like that again.

When she could speak there was a quiver in her voice.

"I left right afterward and never went back. I worked summers and attended UBC and I never shifted into a wolf. Missy and I kept in touch via email and phone, especially after Mom and Dad died in a car accident, but I refused to physically go back to Whistler. Every now and then I'd see pack members hanging around outside my classes, like they were keeping track of me." She shuddered. "Once, they tried to get into the apartment I shared with Pam, but I told her they were cousins I didn't want to see, and somehow she got rid of them."

"I knew I liked her for a reason."

She snorted, and wiped at her teary eyes. "Yeah, well, she thinks you're a little freaky. You know, she's about the best friend I've ever had. Brave and loyal, and fearless and fun, all at the same time. So often I wanted to tell her about being a wolf, but I couldn't. I couldn't risk her leaving me."

Erik handed her a hanky, and she wiped her face clean. She settled back into his arms, his comfort healing her pain. They sat together for a long time, Erik rubbing her back and whispering foreign phrases to her. She had no idea what he was saying, but the words soothed her, eased the ragged edges around her heart.

"I can see why being around wolves frightens you. Not only was your Alpha a rotten bastard, the whole pack was diseased."

Maggie ran a hand up his forearm to caress his biceps. Touching him made her feel so much better. "I'm surprised you're not offering to go rip out their throats."

"Oh, I'm thinking about it. But your brother-in-law, Tad, already killed the Alpha who instigated the whole thing. What I plan in retaliation for the others' sins you don't have to know about."

She sat up quickly. "You're not going after them."

"They hurt you, you're my mate. There will be an accounting."

"I didn't tell you this so you'd go off half-cocked killing people."

Erik raised a brow. "Killing them. Okay, I had other things in mind, but now that you mention it—"

"Stop it. It happened a long time ago. It's been seven years."

"Yet you're still hurting. Sounds like I have cause to give them pain."

She opened her mouth to speak and then froze. Oh damn it. *Damn, damn, damn.*

He was right.

Maggie scrambled out of his lap and stared down at his dark eyes in horror. A light bulb went on in her head, and she could clearly see herself in the room again, the wolves still attacking her. It was like she'd locked the door and never let them go.

She paced toward the nearby trees, grappling with the revelation. She'd suffered years of mental pain and confusion. Loneliness like only a pack animal separated from family could experience. Even the physical weakness caused by locking her wolf away—

None of it had been necessary.

She turned to face him. Her gentle giant, staring back with love in his eyes, concern and anger warring in his heart. He'd seen clearly so many times in the past days exactly what she needed. Was it the mate connection that made him able to cut down the walls and help her break free?

Suddenly she knew part of what she needed.

Him.

Two steps forward returned her to where he sat. "This

isn't about them, it's about me." He moved to speak and she held up her hand. "No, wait and listen. It's true, I'm still in pain. I deliberately didn't see any wolves for years. I didn't visit with my sister in person, and I haven't been able to shift to my wolf in forever. They stole a part of me away and I let them. Ah shit, I *let* them."

"Maggie...no, don't blame yourself. They were the ones who were wrong. You did nothing to deserve this."

She shook her head. "Don't you see? That's what I'm saying, I felt I *did* deserve it. It was my fault Missy was trapped, so I let my wolf become trapped as well in punishment. Oh hell, I've been so stupid."

Erik closed his eyes, and she felt the rush of his power flow over her. She gasped at the depth of it, the richness of the sensation soaking into her very pores. When he opened his eyes, he held out his hand and she grabbed it like a lifeline. "Maggie, I don't know what to say. My brilliant plan to show you my wolf and try to ease your fears seems trite and childish as a solution.

"I feel the strength inside you. Your wolf is powerful, and she wants to help you through this. Your heart is so strong, but you've been using your strength to carry a burden that wasn't yours. I meant what I said about not caring if you shift. Only I'd hate to see her trapped forever when together you can be happy again. Truly happy."

"So if tomorrow is a wolf-only challenge, what would you do?" she whispered.

He shrugged. "As far as I'm concerned, we can go home. This is a game, what you're talking about is real life."

Maggie shook her head. "No! If we go home that's another thing they've stolen from me. From the boys, and the pack. No more. I've had enough of them taking my life away. I want to compete, and I want to get my life back on track." Tears filled her eyes again. She dropped to her knees at his feet and clasped his big hands in hers. "Help me."

Erik rubbed his thumb over her knuckles. "I agree you need to take back control of your life, but Maggie..." He cupped her face in his hand. "You've *been* reclaiming your life. Ever since you started back north you've taken charge and made changes. If you can't finish it all in a few days, you're still well on the way. They aren't winning anymore. You're the one in control of the game now. Okay?"

Her heart leapt. It was true. She nodded jerkily.

"Summer solstice is tomorrow. I think that should help." He pulled off his shirt, and her mouth watered. Firm muscles tempted her. Distracted her from the emotional rollercoaster she'd just raced over. The urgent desire to run her tongue over his body chased away all other thoughts.

How had they resisted completing their mating until now? It was another stone to cast at the feet of her tormentors. Then he was naked, every glorious mile of him spread out like a banquet before her.

"I have no idea how this is supposed to help my wolf, but damn you're fine."

He laughed. "You're drooling."

She wiped at her mouth in response, flushing when he laughed again. "Tease."

"I like the look in your eyes."

Maggie lifted her gaze to his. "You're much better looking than TJ. At least to me."

Erik patted the blanket beside him. "I thought I'd change to my wolf, but I want you to be sure you understand it's me, no matter what form I take. If I frighten you, just tell me to shift back and I will."

"I've been around TJ's wolf for three days."

He frowned. "Sweetheart, I hate to remind you, but TJ

is young and not as powerful as you. He's also not nearly as big as I am. When we do have a shifter challenge there will be few wolves my size. If you can get comfortable around me, that's the first step."

Maggie nodded. "Makes sense."

"Touch me."

She ran her hands up his chest, over all that hard muscle and tight skin, leaning closer to brush their lips together. The thrill of connection shook her to the core even as their lips stayed soft and sweet. She took her time, tracing the tattoos on his shoulders and arms, brushing the stiff hair on his head. She stroked her hands down his abdomen, skirting his erection.

Oh heavens. Distraction at its very finest.

"I think I should shift now."

She nodded, unable to tear her eyes away from the evidence of just how much he really wanted her.

"Maggie, did you hear me? I'm going to shift." A tug on her arm made her drag her gaze back to his face. Erik wore a huge grin. "Although that's a very nice expression you've got right now."

"Okay, Wolfman, let me clap for you."

Shimmering light flashed, transposing images registered on her retinas, and Erik lay on the blanket, all claws and black fur and teeth, and for one awful second, her heart stopped. She closed her eyes and felt for him. It was still Erik. Still the same sensation of power rolling off him, the same love and caring being projected. Gentleness mixed with his incredible strength.

Between the two of them, there was nothing they couldn't accomplish.

Suddenly, that was all she needed. The final wall fell.

"Shift. I need to...I want to..."

She waited, shaking with the fever rippling through her veins. Her blouse came off in one motion, her skirt and bits of underwear flying after it. He changed back, his solid body reforming until he lay on the blanket, naked. She leapt on him, into his arms, tears pouring from her eyes.

"What's wrong? I'm sorry, I didn't mean to push you too fast. You don't have to change. Maggie? Why are you naked?"

She sealed her mouth to his, stealing his words, taking his response. She lay skin-to-skin on top of him, his erection pressing against her belly. She wanted him. Needed him desperately, and there was nothing that would stop her.

He rolled them over, pausing before he covered her. He tangled his fingers in her hair, his tongue stroking and dancing with hers. The wind rustled the leaves overhead, swirls of his power wrapping around them. The pulsing beat between her legs jumped in tempo when he dragged a hand down her body and cupped her breast in the palm of his hand.

When he pulled back they both gasped for air. He stroked his thumb around the tender skin of her nipple, circling again and again as he stared into her eyes. "Are you sure? Make no mistake, I love you and I want you, but I will wait until you're really ready. Don't do this to try and convince your wolf to rise. Don't do this unless you mean it."

Maggie brought her hands to cradle his face. He was so damn big it was easy to forget just how tenderhearted he really was. Her wolf danced inside, waiting to be set free. But before she let her out, she wanted to please the woman.

"The mate thing? It's there, I feel the chemistry between us. But my head says I love you as well. My wolf loves you. And now we need to stop talking and I need you inside me. Please."

He closed his eyes, his face tight with restrained desire. "I didn't want this to happen here. In the wilderness, no soft bed. I wanted it to be special."

She slapped his shoulder. "Damn, it is special. It's you, and me and that's—"

He leaned over to consume her.

10

―――――

*S*oft warm skin under his mouth, her scent filling his head. If he never saw another sunrise, just the memory of this moment—his mate accepting him—would keep him warm for the rest of his life.

She caressed his body, her hands tiny against his chest, over his shoulders. Her touch teased and tormented and he slipped a line of kisses down her torso, partly in an attempt to escape to where he could concentrate on her without being distracted. He cupped her breasts in his hands, the dark skin of her nipples crinkling tight as he lapped at them. First one then the other, licking and nipping and sucking until Maggie panted and writhed under him.

"I love the way you taste." He licked her belly button and she laughed, her torso shaking.

"You talk too much."

"Hmm, you think?"

"Oh. Oh. Oh *yes...*"

Erik smiled against her core, his tongue tracing lazy circles around the rigid nub of her clitoris. He continued his assault, his tongue and fingers playing her like an instrument, now fast, now slower. The sounds of delight she made changed with his tempo until she tightened around his fingers, her sheath squeezing the two fingers he'd buried in her depths.

Again and again he lapped at her, lifting her hips high in the air to pull her closer to his eager mouth. The connection between them grew stronger the longer they touched, and the control he'd wound up, tight as a corkscrew, slowly began to unravel. Destiny meant for them to be together, but after hearing her confession he admired her more than ever. She was brave and bright, and she drove him totally and completely mad with lust.

"Erik!"

He stilled his hand where he'd reached under her hips to caress between her cheeks. A light sheen of sweat broke out on her skin and as she lay before him, her body shaking with another orgasm, he'd never seen a more beautiful sight.

"I love you." He lowered her hips to the blanket and crawled over her, needing to taste her lips again. She clung to his neck and attempted to pull their bodies together. He laughed against her mouth, unwilling to crush her with his weight. She arched under him, rubbing their torsos together, stoking his fires hotter. Moisture from her crotch painted his skin and he groaned. *Gotta keep it slow.* No matter how much he wanted to thrust into her, bury himself in her sweetness. He kissed her, anchored on his elbows to keep them apart.

Maggie poked him in the ribs. "You're too big."

"I'm not even touching you yet."

She laughed with delight and pushed him until he sat up. "Nothing wrong with your ego, is there?" She straddled his thighs, her breasts crushed against his chest, the heat of her pussy now lined up properly with his aching shaft. "Missy wondered if we'd have to—"

"I really don't want to talk about your sister right now. Oh damn, Maggie."

She'd maneuvered herself over the crown of his cock and slowly rode him. Each movement of her hips brought him farther into her body, the tight clasp of her sheath wrapping around him like a bit of heaven. He supported her hips and helped her, watching her face carefully.

She kissed his chest as she settled, his entire length buried inside. "You feel so good in me."

He linked his fingers in her hair, tugging her gaze up to his. "Together. Like we were meant to be."

A mischievous smile crossed her face and she grabbed his shoulders, lifting her hips high until his cock clung to her opening. She dropped down, smooth and fast, hard and amazing. Electric tingles started in his spine and spread fingers out to his balls. There was no way he was going to last. Not after waiting almost two weeks, wanting her desperately the whole time.

She rubbed herself against him on every motion, their bodies slick in the heat of the night. The expression on her face fascinated him and he stared as he assisted her sweet assault on his cock. She bit her bottom lip, her breath coming out in panting gasps.

"More. I want more." Her thoughts sounded in his mind, and he hummed with delight.

Tendrils of knowledge twined from her around his heart —the sensations she felt, the emotions racing through her— all of it passing between them as their mate connection bound them together. He reached out to share his love, his passion for her. How proud he was of her strength. How touched at her willingness to trust him. Their bodies meshed as their minds linked.

She cried out, coming around him, and he let go of his control. Locked together they both reveled in the exquisite explosion. He held her close as after-tremors shook her, the heat of their bodies spreading like a cocoon around them.

"Erik? Is it really happening?"

"Oh yeah, sweetheart. It's real and it's right." He brushed a curl back from her face, leaning closer to kiss her again. The sense of completeness was so amazing. All the missing parts of his soul settled into place as memories of the past and dreams for the future passed between them.

The mate connection—linking them intimately. Everything he'd longed for, making him complete, and it had finally happened. He kissed her without stopping, the need to show her his total love and commitment overwhelming him.

She smiled against his lips, their tongues dancing together, a sweet and content exploration now that the fire had flared.

"I love you." He kissed her eyelids and the tip of her nose, and she laughed out loud.

"You talk too much."

He laughed, stroking her back, enjoying the way she nestled against him, warm and satisfied.

"Erik? I love you too."

How could feeling so wonderful make his heart ache?

His anger at what she'd experienced continued to simmer. It would be a long time before he'd be able to forget how broken she'd been by the attack. Her power as a wolf slipped up a notch and she twisted in his arms. She stared at him, determination written all over her face.

He sent her acceptance for who she was, what she was, not only to him but the pack as well. *"You don't have to do this yet."*

She raised a brow. "Scared she's going to outrun you?"

He felt it. As she reached down deep and called up her wolf, joy overflowed her heart. Aching loneliness from being forced down for so many years washed away. Maggie backed from him, her bright eyes watching closely.

"I'm glad you're here. I'm glad we're together for this." As she reached her hands to the sky, a beam of midnight sun broke through the trees to set her skin glowing. She shifted, shimmered, and Erik knelt forward to rejoice as she paced over to him in wolf, her silvery coat gleaming with health. She leaned forward, her tail wagging with delight and he laughed out loud.

"Shall we run, my mate?" Maggie bumped him with her head, wrapping herself around his torso.

He shifted, his wolf eager to meet his counterpart. They stood nose to nose for a moment, sharing their hearts in wolf form. Erik took off at a run, letting Maggie follow him until they reached the far side of the hill. He stepped aside and she took the lead, her joy in her wolf trailing behind her like a bright rainbow.

He threw back his head and howled, letting the whole world know. He had his mate, they were together. Life couldn't get much better than this.

"I CAN'T BELIEVE IT. You hadn't shifted for seven years? Damn. Someone needs their butts whooped." Jared glared into the distance and TJ growled in agreement.

Maggie held up a hand. "Guys. Put your testosterone

back in your pants. I didn't tell you about my issue to get you riled up." She leaned back on Erik's sturdy frame as she faced TJ and Jared. Both the young men's wolves hovered just under the surface, furious for her sake. She tested her fear at the proximity of more wolves, but there was nothing there. Just calm reassurance emulating from Erik like a lifeline. Craning her head back, she blew him a kiss. *"Thank you for letting me do this my way."*

"Sure, but you'd better finish before they shift without meaning to. Jared especially is really pissed off. You've got an admirer I need to worry about?"

She nudged him in the gut. "I thought you boys needed to know. Last night I shifted, and it was glorious. There will be no troubles in the challenge with me running, but I still don't know how I'll feel when faced with a bunch of strange wolves. I don't want you to get upset if I freak out. With the mate connection between me and Erik, I think I have the strength, but you're my pack now too, and I'm trusting you to help me."

TJ grinned at Jared. "I told you so."

"Yeah, yeah. Mr. Sniffy and his Magic Nose have spoken. Hey, congrats on the mate thing." Jared winked at her before breaking into a huge yawn.

She laughed. "I take it you had a good time last night with Miss Norway?"

Jared glared at TJ who shuffled off a few feet. "Well one of us had a good time."

Laughter rumbled against her back. "TJ? You stole Jared's woman? Again?"

Maggie choked. "TJ?"

He managed to look guilty. He shrugged. "Can I help it if the girls all love the underdog?"

A loud bell rang in the distance.

Erik squeezed her for a second before letting go. "There's the call. Leave everything in the room. They said they'd shuttle us back here when the event is done."

~

THEY WERE all gathered at the starting line. Maggie kept Erik between her and the rest of the crowd without even thinking about it. After so many years of avoidance, she wasn't going to be able to change habits overnight. She took a deliberate step forward and caught Erik grinning down at her.

"Well done, love."

She lifted her chin a little higher and turned to listen to the Games Marshal.

"We're starting the event here instead of in town for the sake of the humans. We'd like to thank all of you for the restraint you showed last night while in Dawson. There were only a few comments this morning at the local coffee shops about unusual wolf sightings, so you seem to have managed to keep yourselves under control while in range of cell phones and other recording devices."

Jared nudged TJ, and the two of them snickered.

"What do you think that's about?" Maggie asked.

"I really don't want to know."

"Today's challenge is a foot race. Cross country toward the Dempster Highway. We've got a loop through the Tombstone Mountains, finishing at the Tombstone campground. All the campers are ours, and we've closed the area to hunting for safety's sake. It's an all-out sprint for your wolves. No bonus points available. At the end of this event, we'll calculate the scores and announce the current standings. Final event will be held in two days' time."

All around them teams were stripping and shifting. Maggie watched in morbid fascination, wondering when the sense of utter horror would creep up her spine and throttle her.

It never came. They were only wolves.

She walked boldly toward the nearest team, shaking off Erik's hand. "I need to do this."

Her opponents watched her warily as she stepped into their midst and stood there.

Nothing. They were only...wolves.

She threw back her head and laughed, joy springing up again.

"You want to come and join us, love? I think you're freaking out our opponents, and that's not very sportsmanlike."

Drat, he was right. She bowed politely to the captain of the team, backing away with deference before leaping into Erik's arms. "I can do this. I really and truly can do this."

He patted her cheek. "I knew you could. Now get naked, little wolf, and let's go for a run."

Stripping off her clothes was freeing. Seeing the admiration in her mate's eyes brought even more pleasure. But the sensation of shifting itself was almost orgasmic. Last night she'd been too worried she wouldn't be able to shift, she'd missed the awesome physical rush.

Today she experienced it fully, moaning with delight.

"Are you going to do that every time you shift? Because, holy shit, that was hot..." Erik nudged her flank, and her wolf took control, teasing and rubbing against her mate. *"Whoa, sweetheart. We're in the middle of a contest. Remember? As*

much as I enjoy sex with you, now is not the time. Rein her in."

Maggie dropped her haunches to sit on the grass. TJ and Jared sniffed her before rolling and offering their throats in submission. If there had been time, she would have howled with delight.

The gun went off and they were away, racing shoulder by shoulder through the Yukon scrub. Brush that was thigh high on a human was level with her head, so she trusted Erik and the others as taller wolves to choose the most direct path through the maze of tough tangle.

Suddenly they broke out into the clear, the sky overhead bright blue, not a cloud to be seen. They ran. Side by side, paws and legs flying, heads and torsos almost touching they were so close together.

There was something wonderful in the freedom of running with a pack again. While last night with Erik had been amazing, today was an answer to another part of the puzzle she'd been missing forever. Belonging. Connecting. A part of a greater whole. Maggie's heart pounded in time with their paws on the ground, eating up the miles.

Ahead she scented the trail they followed. The more time passed, the clearer it became, almost as if the years of being trapped fell away and musty cobwebs brushed from the corners of her wolf's mind.

They tore down a hill and splashed through a stream at the widest point, spray rising and soaking their fur. The fresh, crisp air and the bright green growth teased and inspired her senses to greater heights. Ahead, Erik led the way.

Her mate.

Her heart.

She nuzzled his flank with her nose and thrilled at the

connection between them. TJ and Jared fell back slightly, letting her and Erik lead, and the moment became even more incredible.

"You're running well."

"I'm alive. Truly alive." It was all she had to say and it meant the world.

They must have run for an hour before the trail veered to the side, upward, forcing them to push harder as they topped the mountainside. Now there were large boulders blocking their way and the trail grew narrower. The teams of wolves joined together, forced by the narrowing path to fight for dominance. Maggie stuck close to Erik, her heart beating faster as snarls and the clash of teeth rose behind her.

Erik maneuvered her to his left. TJ growled and there was a yipping cry. She glanced over her shoulder to see four large wolves closing in. Jared and TJ had been separated from them, and a raw slash showed on Jared's shoulder.

"Erik?"

"It's the cheaters from the river. Darren never was one to learn easily. Do you mind if I teach him a lesson?"

Fear skittered across her mind, her throat tightening. Darren. The one who'd leered at her.

Then Erik's will soothed her, strengthened her. *"It's not a challenge to the death, but if I don't do something, who will?"*

That was her mate to a fault. How could she not agree when his sense of fair play and justice was so much a part of who he was? She took a centering breath and reluctantly gave the go ahead.

The power within Erik snapped like a live wire, hot and out of control. He turned in one smooth motion and barreled into the leader of the other foursome. They rolled together, stopping with Erik pinning the other wolf to the ground under him.

He held Darren by the throat, growling in triumph.

"That was quick."

"Bullies are usually wimps."

A low rumble to her right brought Maggie's attention snapping back. Two of the wolves from the other team surrounded her, their lips curled to show their bared canines.

Her knees went weak as memories rushed over her. Growls and tearing pain, sleepless nights and nightmares. She wavered for a second.

"Maggie, fight back. You're strong. There is nothing they can do to you."

One of the wolves snapped at her hind leg, and she whirled on him. Pulling herself to her full height, she let her anger and frustration at being cowed rise.

Too many years. She'd had too many years of being the one to run and hide, and she wasn't going to do it again. A scary growling filled her ears, startling her for a moment until she realized it was her making the racket.

She stared the wolf down, pacing forward deliberately.

He retreated, swinging his head to the side, looking for his backup. Maggie lunged at him, batting at his head with the back of her paw. She didn't want to draw blood, just make him stop. How *dare* this team turn what was supposed to be a fun event into something fearful?

Inside her, anger continued to build. It exploded out, her power flying in his face. He dropped to his belly in an instant and cowered in submission. Turning to face the other wolf, she discovered he'd disappeared under TJ and Jared.

Erik howled once, a long low cry that filled the

mountaintop with his power. Darren sulked off as Erik rose to stride toward her.

Jared licked at his shoulder and she joined him, knocking him to the ground with her body so she could look over the wound. The scratch wasn't too bad, so she let him up, reassuring him with a touch of her nose to his chin.

Erik stroked her muzzle with his. *"Thank you, Beta, for helping care for our pack."*

The lump in her throat felt very strange in wolf form. *"Shit."*

He gave a wolfie chuckle. *"You just realized that now? Yup. You and me, second in command. So what do you say we get running? No one else is going through the pass until we get started and if we sit here too long the people at the finish area are going to wonder what's happened."*

She remained immobile, confused by his words. *"No one else?"*

He bumped her gently, turning her to face down the hillside they'd ascended before the attack. The rest of the competitors lay huddled in groups on the rocky ground, all eyes watching them intently. Darren and his team sat forlornly at the extreme edge of the gathering, dust covered and looking whipped.

She considered for a moment. *"Are they waiting for us to go first?"*

TJ's tail beat the ground so hard dust swirled into the air around them, and Erik nudged him to get him to stop. Maggie threw back her head and howled with delight.

Her wolf was awake, she was whole again, and she and her team had just been honoured by an entire group of wolves.

When the echoes of all the responding cries stopped ringing off the sheer rock cliffs around them, she rose, Erik and the boys joining her. They turned and ran, following the trail to the finish line.

Maggie couldn't care less about the Games. She'd already won the greatest prize imaginable, and he ran beside her all the way.

11

———

"I can't believe you guys got disqualified from the final event. You were in second place headed into it." Keil sighed in disgust.

They were back in Haines, sitting on the front porch of Tad's house, while Jared and TJ stood on the front lawn arguing. Jared was hobbling around on crutches.

Erik laughed. "There's something in the rules that says competitors with broken legs are not eligible, no matter how fast we heal. When the idiot got hit by a car while gawking at the ladies en route to the challenge, there was no way to explain to the human authorities Jared didn't need to go to the hospital. It's okay, everyone was impressed we had the most clues after acing the Peter-and-the-wolf thing. And that trophy we got for being the most sportsmanlike team isn't bad."

"It's a damn big trophy—looks great in the pack house. The old timers were thrilled to see it."

Tad drove up and rolled down his window. "Have you guys seen Jamie? Missy wants me to bring him to the hospital to meet the babies."

125

Erik rose from his chair. "He's with Maggie in the kitchen. I'll go get them."

He rounded the corner, following the invisible connection he had with his mate. The sensation made him smile. He always knew where she was, but more importantly, now *she* knew she was right where she was supposed to be.

With him.

They were fixing up his house, Maggie adding touches. The satisfaction of making those decisions together met a great need in him.

Jamie raced past, his fat little legs pumping wildly.

"You can outrun your mama, but you can't outrun me." Maggie scooped up the squealing toddler, tossing him into the air before catching him and tickling him. His laughter filled the room.

Erik leaned against the wall, soaking it all in.

She glanced at him, eyes bright with love. "I knew you were there."

"Unca Eri." Jamie squealed louder. He squirmed out of her arms and attacked Erik's leg, his pudgy fingers grasping the cotton fabric of his pants and leaving sticky smears behind.

Maggie giggled behind her hand as he picked the little tyke up and poked him in the belly, and more laughter escaped.

Erik beamed at her. "You want to go visit Missy and the girls? Tad's taking Jamie."

Maggie raised her brows. "Hmm, that means the place will be empty." She winked. "I think I should stay here, just in case anyone needs something. I can...guard the house."

"Oh." He transferred the toddler to his other arm and held out his hand to her. She cuddled in close, rubbing against his chest. "You need a hand? With the guarding? It's a big house, with lots of bedrooms."

"Uh-huh. I could use a little backup."

They grinned at each other.

Erik cleared his throat. "By the way. Pam left another bunch of phone messages for you. You'd better call her soon and let her know we didn't bury your body in the bush."

Maggie laughed. "You really okay with inviting her to visit? It's going to make things awkward, since no one will be able to shift while she's around."

He shrugged. "People can deal. In the meantime..." He squeezed her tight for a second, adjusted little Jamie in his arms, and led them off in search of Tad. "We have someone to deliver to his daddy, and then you and I, little wolf, have a date."

She tugged his hand until he bent over far enough for her to press a kiss on his cheek. "I love you. I'm so glad I was brave enough to come north again."

"I love you too, and you're brave enough to face a whole pack of wolves. Even one as big as me."

EPILOGUE

$\mathcal{M}$aggie finally understood that expression "snug as a bug in a rug".

While she was most definitely a wolf and not an insect, she was so completely and enthusiastically comfortable at the moment, even the *thought* of moving seemed like too much work.

Her mate had wrapped an arm around her as usual, holding her tightly against the wall that was his naked body. One leg tucked between hers, his chin resting on her head. She was enveloped and wrapped up as tightly as any Christmas present.

After nearly two months, she was getting to know her mate's habits. Usually Erik was the first to wake, rolling out of bed before her to put on the coffee and get some online work out of the way.

She'd stumble into the kitchen an hour or two later to be greeted by the scent of caffeine, her mate holding out an enormous cup of the elixir of the gods. Sometimes she even got to drink the full cup before the lazy, dirty looks he'd give her from a few feet away would be too much temptation to resist, and they'd end up naked all over again.

Today Maggie had too much to be excited about to sleep in. Even as delectable as her position was. It was an important day, and they had a lot to do...

The thought of how they usually spent their mornings, though, made her hesitate from throwing back the blankets and rushing forward.

Her *mate*.

How utterly wonderful it was to have him curled around her, so gentle in spite of his enormous size. It wasn't just physically that he was big. His heart was three times the size of your average wolf's as well, and all hers.

Hmmmmmm...

Okay, she loved his heart being hers, and his sweet sense of humour, but she liked it all—his bigness, *every*where. Her cheeks heated at the thought of all that bigness...

That wild part inside her rose to the surface in agreement. *Mate—playtime?*

Maggie discovered she was grinning from ear to ear. *Don't mind if I do.*

Erik held her carefully, but he still had one hand cupping her breast. And as it was nearly morning, other parts of his anatomy were waking up.

Should she let the man sleep a few more minutes, or not?

Decisions. Decisions.

Maggie adjusted her hips slightly. Yup. Erik was at least *partially* awake.

She hummed in anticipation, rolling in his arms to press their fronts firmly together. The thick length of him cradled against her belly, and she slid a hand between them and gently teased with her palm.

His eyes remained closed, but his lips curled in a smile. "Don't wake me. I'm having this really awesome dream."

She brushed her lips over his, still stroking. "Is it a *dirty* dream?"

"Oh, yeah."

"Good. We must be having the same one," she whispered, pushing on his shoulder.

He rolled to his back, taking her with him, and for the next while things got nice and hot *and* dirty, just the way they both liked it.

A seemingly long while later they lay side by side, fingers linked, chests still heaving from their exertions. Pleasure beyond the physical connected them.

"*I love you,*" Erik stated plainly, straight into her mind. "*I know we're mates already. I didn't think we really needed more, but we do. It's good for the pack to come together to celebrate, but I'm looking forward to it as well. It's another memory for us. This wedding thing.*"

Maggie rolled to her side, laughing as she pushed up far enough to hover over him. "I'm glad you came to this conclusion, considering we're doing this 'wedding thing' today."

He grinned lazily. "I just wanted you to know it's not just to make you happy. I want this too."

She laid a hand on his chest and leaned in to kiss him, dodging back when he would've pulled her in for another round of sexy entanglement.

"Not until tonight," she scolded. "There's still things to prepare, and Pam is arriving in an hour."

Erik brushed a finger over her cheek. "You've missed her."

"She's my best friend," Maggie said. "And one of the most kick-ass women ever."

"Human. Who's about to walk, unknowingly, into the midst of a wolf pack."

She shrugged. "She'll be fine. I have great taste in friends and mates."

"Can't argue with that," he agreed. "Fingers crossed no one walks naked through the pack house and freaks her out."

They grinned at each other. As special as the day was going to be, she'd already given her heart, soul, and *everything* to the beautiful man looking up at her with love in his eyes.

They settled in the kitchen, coffee finally filtering into her system when there was a knock and a familiar dark-haired figure stuck his head through the doorway.

"Heads up, love birdies. Ready for your big day?" TJ flashed his perfectly white grin set in a gorgeous face.

"Call me a birdie again, and you'll learn to fly," Erik offered smoothly, playing his fingers over Maggie's where they lay linked on the table.

She snickered then gestured to an empty chair. "Want to come in?"

TJ stepped through the doorway, but shook his head. "I've been told in no uncertain terms not to bother you for long, but I thought you'd like to know—we got a call at the pack house. Pam's flight is going to be about an hour late."

Shoot. Maggie fought to keep her disappointment from showing. "Okay. That still puts her here in plenty of time."

"Who's picking her up?" Erik asked. "I thought you and Jared would be at the airport already."

TJ looked sheepish. "We missed the departure time, so Mark Weaver went without us."

"TJ." Erik folded his arms, and it was his turn to look disappointed.

"Hey, this time it wasn't...*entirely*...my fault." TJ sealed his lips and refused to say anything else, which Maggie thought was pretty decent of him, considering disasters often were his fault.

"We'll be over to the pack house in a few minutes," Erik informed him, then offered a happier expression. "Thanks for agreeing to be our best man."

TJ damn near glowed, straightening up and looking a lot more like his big brother, the Alpha, than he usually did. "I won't mess up, I promise."

"You'll do great," Maggie assured him. "And I'm looking forward to hearing you play for us at the reception. Our favourites, yes?"

He laughed softly. "John Denver and Bon Jovi. You guys are hysterical, you know that, right?"

"Hey, be glad I didn't ask for the theme song from the Friendly Giant," Erik deadpanned.

TJ's grin widened. He tipped an imaginary hat and began whistling as he backed toward the door, preparing to leave.

Maggie laughed as she recognized the tune from the old time children's show, then sucked in a gasp as TJ turned and bounced off the doorframe. He adjusted position and carried on with only a second's hiccup in the music.

She and Erik glanced at each other and smiled, which turned into laughter, which turned to full out gasps before they were done.

"He's a good guy," Erik said, wiping tears from his eyes. "He is."

"I agree." But he was...*TJ*. There was a certain rightness in knowing that as much as things changed, things stayed the same.

TJ had a charm that was all his own.

She got up from the table and slipped into Erik's lap, best men and bride's maids temporarily forgotten. "It appears I have about an hour to burn..."

Erik's eyes lit up.

Yup—it was going to be a great day. She pressed her lips to his and started on another round of memories.

~

No way were they going to survive this.

TJ glanced over his shoulder, ruefully wondering exactly what the punishment might be for mucking up the pack Betas' wedding day.

Maybe Erik would be too distracted to notice. Maybe Maggie would decide they didn't really need a wedding cake. Maybe Jared would keel over dead in the middle of the hall right before the bride and groom went to cut the cake and discovered the disaster.

That one TJ could picture vividly, heck, he could arrange it—Jared, keeling over, dead. That would be *juuuuust* fine right about now.

"I can't believe you were so stupid." TJ swore long and hard, hands shaking as he paced the massive cold room off the pack house kitchen. The same place he'd been delayed when he and Jared were supposed to be meeting with Mark to go grab Pam from the airport.

The shelves were lined with stacks of prepared trays— wolf appetites were legendary. Chicken wings, sliders, coconut shrimp, and piles and piles of steaks waited to be put on the barbeques and grilled.

The desserts arranged on the other side of the room were just as impressive. All except for the one set carefully at the far corner of the room. The one that even to TJ looked like it was important. Tall, thick, covered in white icing...with an enormous chunk missing front and center. A triangle with rough edges, and maybe a few finger-shaped imprints.

TJ blinked hard then checked again, hoping the original damage he'd seen wasn't as bad as he thought. Actually, it wasn't.

It was worse.

Jared leaned on the wall, casually eating a cold hamburger patty. "If I can point out—*you* told me to 'grab a bite'. That there were a trillion things to eat in here, and it was like food heaven."

TJ pinched the bridge of his nose and suddenly understood why his brother often looked as if he was one step away from developing an ulcer.

Wolves were a pain in the ass.

"There *are* a trillion things to eat. So why the hell did you put your paw into the one thing you shouldn't touch?"

"It was dark."

Another spike of pain shot through TJ. "*Why* was it dark?"

Jared indicated the switch in the middle of the wall to the left of the door. "It got bumped off."

"Death is going to be too good for you," TJ warned his friend.

"Cheryl's back hit it," Jared admitted. "We got a little vigorous, and the next thing I knew it was dark, and she was howling and—"

TJ held up a hand. "I don't need the details of your latest conquest, man. Just, did you *have* to have a snack while still in the dark? You couldn't open the door or something?"

Jared finally had the grace to look embarrassed. "Turns

out she likes it in the dark. Who am I to deny a woman her heart's desire?"

"Or any other part of her?" TJ ignored his friend and went to examine the damages again. "Maybe if we..."

He twisted the cake sideways. Then the other direction.

Nope. The only thing making this look better was a blow torch or a shovel.

Shovel.

TJ eyed the scooped out section again, then glanced around at the goodies filling the room, sudden hope hitting hard. "Okay, this might not be the last day of our lives. Grab me a spoon or something, and bring me the stuff I ask for. And hurry, we don't have much time."

It was a miracle in the first place that no one interrupted them. It was a miracle that TJ didn't accidentally have his hands slip at the wrong moment, but somehow he managed to stay coordinated enough to finish the task and carefully back away, pushing Jared to a safe distance as well.

Jared shook his head in amazement. "Incredible. I'd never have come up with that."

"Desperate times, man." TJ stared down at his handiwork.

He'd scooped out more of the cake, rounding the corners a little to create a deeper hole in the side. Outside the "cave" he'd placed a couple brownies and a pile of sugar cookie pieces, both stacked in a way they mostly resembled small wolfish figurines—one dark brown larger, the white one more petite. Between them he'd built a fire of chocolate covered pretzel sticks, with red and yellow cupcake icing dabbled on top for flames.

He shared the extra cupcake leftovers with Jared, and the two of them ate quietly as they eyed his creation.

"It's not bad," TJ said finally.

"Not bad at all." Jared offered a fist bump. "Now, I'll go find the chef and duct tape her to something before she sees the changes and has a bird."

Tempting.

"You should bribe her," TJ offered instead. "Someone would probably notice if she went missing."

Jared considered. "She is pretty hot. I could handle that."

TJ rolled his eyes. "Is everything about sex to you?"

His friend shook his head for a moment before the motion slowed then reversed direction to a nod.

They grinned at each other.

"Hey." Jared shrugged. "I'm a healthy young wolf in the prime of life. Who am I to deny the world my amazingness."

TJ pretended to stick his finger down his throat. "Well, you take care of the chef. I have Maggie's friend to look after."

Jared snorted. "Have fun with that. Babysitting the human. Poor man—you'll be getting sex...never?"

Whatever. TJ shoved his friend out the door, one final glance to make sure the cake looked respectable as it could. "Not everything is about sex," he muttered. "Friendship is important."

"You keep telling yourself that. Maybe Mark will hit it off with her, and you won't have to mind her all night."

Whatever. He patted his friend on the shoulder, hard, then headed toward the back of the house where his stuff waited. It was time to grab a shower and get ready. This was a big day for his friends, and no matter what he was going to make sure they had a great time, including the human BFF.

And who knew? Maybe in the middle of being all responsible and shit, he'd have a good time as well.

There really was no knowing what surprises the day would bring.

~

New York Times Bestselling Author Vivian Arend
brings you a series of light-hearted,
stand-alone novellas, with fated mates and always a
happily-ever-after.

~

Granite Lake Wolves
Wolf Signs
Wolf Flight
Wolf Games
Wolf Tracks
Wolf Line
Wolf Nip

~

ABOUT THE AUTHOR

New York Times and *USA Today* bestselling author Vivian Arend loves to share the products of her over-active imagination with her readers. She writes contemporary, western, and light-hearted paranormal romances. The stories are humorous yet emotional, usually with a large cast of family or friends, and a guaranteed happily-ever-after.

Vivian lives in British Columbia, Canada, with her husband of many years—her inspiration for every hero and a willing companion for all sorts of adventures.

Find out more at www.vivianarend.com.

www.ingramcontent.com/pod-product-compliance
Lightning Source LLC
Chambersburg PA
CBHW031002210726